Millions of readers!

FOR ALMOST FIFTY YEARS Americans have followed and enjoyed the adventures of Dick Tracy. Over five hundred newspapers carry the famous comic strip, and millions of people read it every day. Now this fast, action-filled powerhouse of a novel captures the thrilling adventures of America's favorite detective—the one and only Dick Tracy!

DICK TRACY

William Johnston

BERKLEY BOOKS, NEW YORK

DICK TRACY

PRINTING HISTORY
Tempo edition / June 1970
Published simultaneously in Canada
Berkley edition / August 1990

For information address: The Berkley Publishing Group,
200 Madison Avenue, New York, New York 10016.

ISBN: 0-425-12742-7

A BERKLEY BOOK ® TM 757,375
Berkley Books are published by The Berkley Publishing Group,
200 Madison Avenue, New York, New York 10016.
The name "BERKLEY" and the "B" logo
are trademarks belonging to Berkley Publishing Corporation.

PRINTED IN THE UNITED STATES OF AMERICA

10 9 8 7 6 5 4 3 2 1

DICK TRACY

One

THE SLEEK black police car equipped with built-in roll bars eased smoothly through the city traffic, carrying Dick Tracy and his fellow detective, Sam Catchem, on a more or less routine mission. They seemed disturbed, however. Tracy's eyes were narrowed into a squint. Sam's chipmunk face was fixed in a dark scowl. They were thinking the same thing—that there was more to the assignment than was showing on the surface.

Sam finally spoke. "Tracy—do you think the Chief is right?"

Tracy glanced at him, then turned his eyes back to the traffic. "About Dr. Zgani? It wouldn't be the first time a man was reported missing, then turned up. It happens a lot. People have a lot of personal reasons for wanting to drop out of sight temporarily. The Chief thinks that's what happened in Dr. Zgani's case—and he's probably right."

"But Zgani isn't just anybody," Sam pointed out. "He's one of this country's top scientists. Why would a man like that want to disappear?"

"Scientists are human beings," Tracy smiled. "They have the same human problems we all have. So it's just as logical for a scientist to need to get away for a few hours as anyone else."

"But, according to the report, he admits he was gone, but he doesn't remember being anywhere. How do you figure that?"

"Isn't it possible that he doesn't want us—or anyone—to know where he was?"

"Right—and that's what bothers me," Sam said. "As I understand it, Zgani is in charge of a number of secret government projects. How do we know that, while he was gone, he wasn't selling the secrets he knows to some foreign government?"

"Think, Sam. If you were selling secrets to a foreign agent, would you do it in a way that would draw attention to yourself? Dr. Zgani's sudden disappearance—and then his equally sudden reappearance—has created a lot of concern. We're looking into it, and the F.B.I. is looking into it, and probably a number of other government agencies—ones that we don't even know about—are poking into it, too. Does a traitor go out of his way to get himself investigated?"

"Then you think it's something simple and innocent?"

Tracy frowned thoughtfully, but did not reply.

"Tracy?" Sam prodded. "Is that what you think it is, something innocent?"

"We're here," Tracy said, turning the car into a drive that led to a huge complex of low, red brick buildings.

The complex was a government laboratory. A moment later the car reached a guard post. The Marine on duty checked their identification, then pointed out the building in which they would find Dr. Victor Zgani.

They parked the car, then entered the building, where they were halted by another guard. After having had their identification checked a second time they were directed down a long corridor to a door that had the doctor's name on it. Beyond the door they found a small reception room and a middle-aged female secretary. She escorted them into Dr. Zgani's private office.

Dr. Zgani rose from behind his desk. He was a small, fragile-looking man with close-cropped white hair and deep wrinkles in his face. He did not seem especially pleased to see them.

"I hope this won't take too much time," he said, offering them chairs. "I've been questioned until I'm beginning to doubt my story myself. Meanwhile, my work isn't getting done."

"We'll be as brief as we can," Tracy smiled, settling into a chair. "But, try to understand, Doctor. You possess a lot of important information. Anything that happens to you is of concern to a great many people."

Dr. Zgani nodded irritably. "Yes, yes, I know." He sat down behind his desk again. "Well, how do you want it—from the beginning? There isn't much to tell. The night before last, I left the laboratory, headed for home. I'd worked late, it was about nine o'clock. I checked out through all the guard posts. Then—"

"That was Tuesday night, right?" Sam broke in.

"Uh . . . yes, Tuesday night. I left here and drove directly home. And when I reached there my house was swarming with government people and my wife was on the verge of hysterics and I was told that I had been missing for something like twenty-four hours. I was baffled. I couldn't believe it. I still find it very, very difficult to believe. But apparently it's true."

"Who . . . when was it discovered that you were missing?" Tracy asked.

"When I hadn't reached home at midnight—that was still Tuesday—my wife telephoned here, the laboratory. She was told that I had left a little after nine.

Well, it's only about a thirty-minute drive from here to my home. So, she became alarmed. She contacted you people, the police. And someone in your organization apparently called in the government people."

"It was Wednesday night—a little after nine—when you reached home, is that correct?" Tracy said.

Dr. Zgani nodded.

"And you have no knowledge, no recollection, no awareness at all of where you were during those twenty-four hours from Tuesday night until Wednesday night?"

"None. Absolutely none. All I know is that I got into my car and drove home, and that somewhere along the way I lost twenty-four hours."

"Did you make any stops along the way?" Tracy asked.

"Only at the traffic signals."

"You didn't leave your car?"

Dr. Zgani shook his head. "Except at the gate," he said.

"The gate?"

"My house is in the hills " he explained, "and the property is ringed by a fence. There's a gate and it has to be opened and closed to get the car through it. I got out of the car to open the gate, but that's all."

"Do you have any idea what could have happened to you, Doctor?" Tracy asked.

"Some form of amnesia, that's the best guess I can make," he replied. "Evidently my mind went blank. I must have been driving around for twenty-four hours. I've been working very hard lately, long hours. My mind, I suppose, must have rebelled. It must have decided that it needed a rest."

"And played hooky for twenty-four hours," Sam said.

"Yes. That's the only explanation I can offer." He suddenly looked grim. "No one seems to believe that. I get the impression that the government men suspect that I spent those missing twenty-four hours with some foreign spy. But that's preposterous. If I wanted to—" He snorted. "It's just preposterous, that's all."

"Did you feel that your mind needed a rest?" Tracy asked.

Dr. Zgani was silent for a moment, frowning thoughtfully. "Actually, no. I'm working on some pretty exciting things. I haven't felt tired. On the contrary, I've been stimulated. But, then, the brain is a very complex, a very sophisticated organ. It's possible that it knew more about my physical and mental condition than I did." He shrugged. "I have no other explanation."

Tracy rose. "Thank you, Doctor. We won't take up any more of your time—not at the moment, anyway."

"But if you think of anything," Sam said, rising too, "you call us, will you?"

Dr. Zgani gestured vaguely, signifying nothing.

Tracy and Sam left the laboratory.

As they drove back toward headquarters, Sam said, "Do you believe it? Was he just driving around?"

"It's possible," Tracy replied.

"But do you believe it?"

Tracy shook his head. "I tend to believe *him,* though—that he doesn't know where he was. However, that isn't much help. It doesn't explain what happened."

"We may never know," Sam said.

"Do we have his address—his home address?" Tracy asked.

Sam picked up a file folder that was lying on the seat beside him and opened it and thumbed through the papers in it. "Here it is," he replied. "It's up on Sycamore Woods Road. Do you want to talk to his wife?"

Tracy shook his head. "I'd like to look at that gate," he said.

They reached Sycamore Woods Road about a quarter of an hour later. It wound up through the hills. On either side of the road was thick forest. Eventually they reached the gate. They could see the house—a large, white, stucco, two-story structure—about a quarter of a mile beyond it.

Tracy and Sam got out of the car. Tracy stood looking at the gate speculatively, as if hoping it might speak to him and explain the mystery.

"It's just a gate," Sam said.

Tracy nodded and sighed puzzedly. Then he glanced about. The road continued past Dr. Zgani's property, winding on up into the hills.

"Let's follow it," he said.

"What for? It's just a road."

"A hunch," Tracy replied.

They got back into the car and drove slowly along the road.

"What are we looking for?" Sam asked.

"I don't know."

"Great—then how will we know if we see it?"

"There!" Tracy said, pointing. "A car has pulled off into the woods. See the tracks?"

"So?"

"I don't know."

About a half-mile further on, the road came to a dead-end. Tracy turned the car around, then headed back, driving slowly again.

"There aren't any other houses up here," he said. "Why would anybody drive a car up here?"

"Beats me," Sam replied.

"But somebody did. Somebody drove a car up here and parked it in the woods. Who? Why?"

When they reached the spot where the tracks led into the woods, Tracy stopped the car and they got out again. They inspected the area, but they found nothing but the tracks.

"What are you getting at, Tracy?" Sam said, baffled. "Are you trying to say that Zgani drove his car up here and parked? For twenty-four hours? That doesn't make any sense at all. Why would he do a thing like that?"

"I didn't say that he did," Tracy replied. "I'm just curious about why a car would be here. Can you explain it?"

"Somebody was lost."

"The tracks go too far into the woods—as if somebody wanted to hide the car."

"That gets us right back to Zgani. Was he hiding? What for? What from?"

Tracy shook his head. "I just don't know, Sam. But there's one thing I *am* sure of—I don't think this case is either simple or innocent any more."

Driving back toward headquarters, Tracy and Sam received a call on the car radio. It was an urgent message from the Chief to report to him as soon as possible. They reached headquarters a few minutes later. It was mid-afternoon by then. They hurried directly to the Chief's office.

"What did you find out from Dr. Zgani?" the chief asked.

"Nothing that was much help—so far," Tracy replied.

"Maybe this is going to tie-in with it," the Chief said. "Have you ever heard of Theodore Mansard?"

"The historian?" Tracy replied. "Of course."

"Even I've heard of him," Sam said. "And, I'll tell you the truth, I don't keep up much on historians."

"He's missing," the Chief continued. "At least, we think he's missing. He left his home this morning. He was headed for the University. The historical Society was having a luncheon and Professor Mansard was supposed to be the speaker. But he didn't show up. Nobody has seen him. He's vanished."

"Who reported it?" Tracy asked.

"His housekeeper. She got a call from somebody at the Historical Society—they were wondering what had happened to Mansard. She knew that he should have arrived long before that, so she called the hospitals, thinking he might have been in an accident. But nothing. So she telephoned us. And that's about where it stands."

"What does it have to do with Zgani?" Sam asked.

"Two famous men," the Chief replied. "A famous scientist and a famous historian. We get a lot of missing persons reports every day, but how often do we get them on famous men?"

"I suppose there *could* be a connection," Sam said. "But—"

"I think we better check it out," Tracy said. "What's been done, so far, Chief?"

"I sent some men to the Professor's house, and some others to the University. I don't have a report from any of them yet."

"Do we have a detail sheet?"

The Chief handed Tracy a sheet of yellow paper. "Here's everything we have. There's a description of his car and his license number there. There's an all-points out on it. But it hasn't been spotted."

Taking the copy of the detail sheet with them, Tracy and Sam left headquarters and drove to Professor Mansard's home. When they arrived, a detective from Missing Persons was questioning the housekeeper. They listened. But they did not learn any more. All she could tell the detective was that the Professor had left for the University and had failed to arrive.

They drove next to the University. There they found another detective from Missing Persons questioning the head of the Historical Society. But he had no information of any significance to offer either.

Stymied, Tracy and Sam returned to the parking lot, where they had left the car. Tracy radioed to headquarters and spoke to the Chief. But the Chief had nothing new to report.

"Let's drive back along the route between here and the Professor's house," Tracy said.

"We've been that way once."

"All right, we'll drive it again. Maybe we missed something."

"There's no woods for him to hide in, I'll tell you that," Sam said gruffly.

As Tracy was backing the car out, he suddenly put on the brakes. "Over there!" he said, pointing along the line of cars in the lot. "Isn't that his car?"

Sam checked the detail sheet. "That's it! Same make, same model, same license number."

Tracy parked again, then they got out and hurried to the Professor's car. It was vacant. They opened the doors and looked in. There was no sign of anything out of order.

"We better get the fingerprint boys over here," Sam said.

"Not yet," Tracy replied. "Sam, go to my lab. On my workbench, you'll find a machine. It's portable. Bring it back here."

"What is it?" Sam asked.

"It's a thermo-sensitive camera."

Sam rolled his eyes. "I won't even ask what *that* is," he said.

When Sam departed, Tracy moved back from the car. He sat on a bench, thinking, puzzling. And he was still there, deep in thought, when Sam returned.

"Is this it?" Sam asked, handing a fair-sized but light-weight, complicated-looking machine to Tracy. "You'll pardon me for asking, but I wouldn't know a thermo-whatchamacallit from a bag of bananas."

"That's it," Tracy smiled.

He took the camera to the car and began pressing the shutter, photographing from different angles.

"Pictures?" Sam said. "Why don't you just let the lab boys do that?"

"This isn't an ordinary camera, Sam. It photographs body heat."

"It what?"

"Body heat. A person's body gives off heat—you know that, don't you?"

"Sure. But whose body heat are you photographing? There's nobody there."

"When a person is in a certain place for a while—minutes or even seconds—his body heat, naturally, is concentrated in that spot. When he moves on, he leaves a deposit of body heat. And it lingers for a while."

Sam looked doubtful. "Are you kidding me?"

"You'll see—after I develop this film," Tracy replied.

"You mean I'll *see* body heat?"

"In a sense."

"And when I see it, what will it tell me?" Sam asked. "Is this a talking picture you're taking? Will the body heat tell me where the Professor has gone?"

Tracy laughed. "Not quite." He headed back toward his own car. "Let's call the Chief and tell him what we've found," he said.

A few minutes after Tracy had reported to the Chief, a squad car arrived. It carried a lab man and a uniformed officer. The man from the police laboratory began going over the Professor's car for evidence of someone else's presence.

"I'm to take the car to the headquarters garage," the uniformed officer said to Tracy. "Are you finished with it?"

"Yes—but let's leave the car right where it is," Tracy replied. "I want you to stay here, too. Keep an eye on the car. Who knows?—the Professor may show up here."

The officer saluted, then returned to the squad car.

Tracy and Sam drove to Tracy's lab. There, Tracy developed the film he had taken, then placed the positive prints on a lighted screen.

"Ghosts!" Sam said. "All you got was ghosts."

"Those ghosts are concentrations of body heat," Tracy explained. "Do you understand now why I wanted to photograph the car?"

Sam shook his head. "I wouldn't even try to guess."

"Count the hot spots," Tracy said.

"The what?"

"The ghosts."

"Oh. Okay. One . . . two . . . three . . . four . . . five . . . Five—that's all."

"And how many can you account for? How many people have been near the car, as far as we know?"

"Well, let's see . . . you, me, the fingerprint guy—"

"No, no," Tracy broke in. "I took the photos before the man from the lab arrived."

"Yeah, that's right. So, that leaves you, and me and the Professor. That's three. But there're five— Yeah . . . now I get it. Two of those hot spots don't belong there."

"Right. It isn't the kind of evidence that would hold up in court, but it's something for us to work on," Tracy said. "It's a pretty good indication that Professor Mansard didn't just wander away—that he was taken away."

"By two men."

"By two *persons*."

"Where does it get us?" Sam asked.

"I'm not sure," Tracy frowned. "When I took those pictures, I didn't expect to find those two other hot spots. I thought we would find that Professor Mansard had left the car of his own free will. That would link his disappearance—in a superficial way, at least—with Dr. Zgani's. Understand what I'm getting at?"

"Not exactly," Sam replied.

"Well, as far as we know, Dr. Zgani wasn't abducted. There was no one else involved in the disappearance—right?"

"He didn't see anybody, at least—so he says."

"And, if we hadn't found those two extra hot spots near Professor Mansard's car, we could assume that he wasn't abducted either," Tracy continued.

"But the ghosts change all that. In other words, there isn't any connection between the two cases," Sam said.

"That's what I was thinking—until a couple seconds ago," Tracy replied. "But then I realized that my theory has some holes in it—one big hole in particular. I don't have heat sensitive photographs of Dr. Zgani's car just after he disappeared to compare with the photographs of Professor Mansard's car. If I did have, I might find extra hot spots in them too. And that would indicate that the Chief's guess is right—that there is a connection between the two cases.

Sam shook his head. "Hold it—you're just confusing me more."

"Well, anyway, the important thing now is to find Professor Mansard," Tracy said. "Let's go back to his house and talk to his housekeeper. Maybe we can get something from her that will give us a better lead than we have now."

Sam grunted. "It wouldn't have to be much to beat what we have to work on so far," he said. "A guy parks his car and then vanishes into thin air. That's not much better than nothing."

Tracy frowned. "Parked his car . . ." he mused.

"What'd I say?"

"Nothing, probably. Forget it." He headed toward the door. "Let's go. I have a feeling that we're going to have to do a lot of digging to get the answer to *this* puzzle."

Two

THE TALK with Professor Mansard's housekeeper yielded nothing that was of any significance. When Sam and Tracy went off duty that night they had a feeling of total defeat.

The next morning they resumed the investigation, systematically questioning all of the Professor's close friends and acquaintances. They found out that he was well-liked as a person, highly-respected in his field, and far from wealthy. The information appeared to rule out a kidnapping—there was no motive.

Late in the afternoon they checked in with the Chief by radio. Tracy asked if there had been any action at the Professor's abandoned car. He was advised that there had not been, but that the stake-out was being continued.

"Let's drive over there and look at that car again," Tracy said to Sam. "Maybe we missed something.

As they drove toward the University, Sam said, "It's been about twenty-four hours since he disappeared. That's how long Dr. Zgani was gone. If there's any connection—in that way—between the two cases, the Professor ought to be showing up about now."

"I wouldn't count on it," Tracy said. "That would be a bit too much of a coincidence."

As they turned into the University parking lot they saw a crowd of people around Professor Mansard's car.

"There's your action," Sam said.

They parked the car, then ran to where the crowd had collected. In the center of the crush of people they found a uniformed policeman. He was lying on the ground, on his back.

"Give him air—get back!" Sam commanded.

Tracy had bent down to the man. "It's too late for that," he reported. "He's dead." He got to his feet. "Sam—get on the radio. Get an ambulance over here." He gestured to the people. "Get back, please."

As Sam hurried off, Tracy glanced toward the Professor's car. To his surprise, he saw a man seated behind the wheel—white-haired and benevolent-looking—who answered Professor Mansard's description perfectly. At the moment, the man was peering baffledly out the car window at the crowd.

Tracy opened the door. "Professor Mansard?"

"Yes. What the devil's happening here?"

"Can't you tell us?" Tracy asked.

"Tell you? Tell you what? I just drove up and parked here and all of a sudden the car was surrounded by all these people. That policeman—what happened?"

"He was shot. Don't you know anything about it?"

"Nothing . . . nothing . . . absolutely nothing. I have a speaking engagement here. I'm addressing the Historical Society."

At that moment, Sam reappeared. "The ambulance is on—" He interrupted himself, staring at the man in the car. "Is that—"

"It is . . . and he thinks it's yesterday," Tracy replied.

Professor Mansard scowled at him. "I said no such thing."

"Professor, it was yesterday, exactly twenty-four hours ago, that you were scheduled to speak to the members of the Historical Society," Tracy said. "You've been missing. Do you have any idea where you've been?"

"Missing? You're talking absolute nonsense!" Professor Mansard replied curtly. "I left my house a few minutes ago and drove directly here to the University. What do you mean, missing? Is this some sort of joke?"

In the distance there was the sound of an ambulance siren.

"One of our men is dead," Tracy replied. "There's no joke about that. He was watching your car, waiting for you to return. You *did* return—and, as a result, he was killed. Why? Where have you been? Who killed him? We want some answers."

"Preposterous," Professor Mansard said grimly. "Totally preposterous. I won't say another word."

The ambulance arrived and the body of the policeman was taken away. Then, with Professor Mansard in custody, Tracy and Sam set out to prove to him that he had been missing. The three talked to the president of the Historical Society, who assured the Professor that his address had been scheduled for the day before and that he had not appeared. Next, Tracy and Sam took the Professor to his home, where his housekeeper confirmed that he had disappeared and that she had called the police to search for him. The evidence was too strong for the Professor to deny any longer.

"It happened," the Professor admitted when they arrived at headquarters and he was seated in the chief's office. "I don't know how. I don't know why. But, undeniably, it happened."

"Think," Tracy urged. "Try to remember. Did anything—just *anything*—happen that was out of the ordinary?"

"I have no recollection, no recollection at all, of those twenty-four hours," the Professor replied. "I remember leaving my house. I remember the drive to the University. I remember parking my car. And then, as I told you, suddenly there was a crowd around the car and the policeman was lying there dead. But nothing—" He frowned thoughtfully.

"What?" Tracy said.

"I parked the car. I started to get out— But then, later, I don't think he was there. I can't recall seeing him."

"Who?"

"The man with the eye patch. A black eye patch over his right eye. Ugly-looking fellow. As I started to get out of the car, I saw him. And then, later, when the crowd gathered, he was gone. Or, at least, I didn't see him any more. But there were so many people."

"Now, wait a minute," the Chief said. "Was this before or after you disappeared?"

"How can I answer that? I have no rememberance of having been gone."

The Chief punched a button on his intercom system. "Put this through the computer," he said, speaking to an officer in the Records Department. "A man with a black eye patch—right eye, ugly."

"Yes, sir," a voice replied.

"Professor, are you acquainted with Dr. Victor Zgani?" Tracy asked.

"The scientist? No. I know of him, by reputation. But I've never met him."

"Do you know of any connection between him and you?"

"In what way?"

"In any way," Tracy replied.

The Professor scowled, thinking, then shook his head. "No. No, I can't think of any connection at all. Why do you ask?"

"The same thing happened to him—he disappeared for twenty-four hours," Tracy replied. "We managed to keep it quiet, because of his work on some secret government projects. You're not, by any chance, working on any secret government projects, are you?"

The Professor smiled. "If they were secret, I wouldn't be able to tell you. But, no, no I'm not. I'm a historian. What would I be doing for the government?"

The door opened and an officer entered. He was carrying several photographs and he handed them to the Chief. "This is what we got from the computer," he reported.

The Chief thanked him, and the officer left.

"Take a look at these," the Chief said, handing the four photographs to Professor Mansard. "Let's see if your one-eyed man is here."

The Professor accepted the pictures. "Who are these, criminals?"

"They have records," the Chief replied.

The Professor looked through the photographs once, then again, then a third time, then picked one of them and handed it to the Chief. "This might possibly be the man," he said. "I got only a fleeting glimpse of him. I can't be sure."

The Chief looked at the information on the back of the photograph. "Carl 'Dutch' Borgman," he read. He handed the photograph to Sam. "Put out a pick-up on him," he said.

Taking the picture, Sam left the office.

Tracy and the Chief questioned Professor Mansard

for another half-hour or so. But they got nothing from him that appeared to be helpful. After that, Tracy drove the Professor to his home.

When Tracy returned to headquarters he went to the section that housed the computer. He was programming it to do a special job for him when Sam entered.

"Has it come to that?" Sam said. "Are you getting that thing to do your thinking for you?"

"Computers don't think, Sam. They calculate—fast and accurately."

"Do you expect it to tell you where Dr. Zgani and Professor Mansard were for twenty-four hours?"

"No."

"Then what?"

"I'm hoping it will do some correlating for me. I gave it two words—scientist and historian. I'm asking it to give me the third word. We know that a scientist and a historian disappeared. The third word—I hope—will tell us who will disappear next. Or, anyway, who would logically disappear next."

"By name?"

"No, only by occupation. Computers can't do everything."

"Then, I don't see—"

Tracy had punched a button, activating the computer. There was a whirring sound. A number of different colored lights blinked on and off. Typewriter keys clattered. Then the whirring sound ceased.

Tracy read the typed answer that the machine had provided. "Administrator," he said.

Sam groaned. "That's a great help."

Tracy sank into a chair behind a desk and leaned back. "Let's think about it," he said. "Let's assume that Dr. Zgani and Professor Mansard were abducted.

Somehow they were rendered unconscious and taken somewhere and kept there for a period of twenty-four hours. But why? Not for money. There were no ransom notes. And they were released. What was the point of it?"

"We're looking for a nut," Sam decided.

Tracy shook his head. "No. There's a logical and meaningful reason for it. But what? What did the kidnapper have to gain? What did he get? What did the Professor and Dr. Zgani have to give? No money. What do they have? Their knowledge, that's about all they have."

"And they still have it," Sam said.

"Mmmmm . . . they still have it. But . . . who else has it? Knowledge is a thing that can be given away and yet still retained."

Sam squinted at him. "Pardon?"

"When you go to school, you get knowledge from a teacher—right? But the teacher doesn't lose that knowledge, he still has it."

"Yeah, I suppose so," Sam nodded. "But how could somebody get Zgani's and Mansard's knowledge without them knowing about it? It doesn't make any sense, Tracy."

"It doesn't make any sense because we don't have all the answers yet." Tracy sat up. "Now, the next question is, why would anybody want the Professor's and the Doctor's knowledge?"

"We know why somebody might want Zgani's," Sam replied. "Those secret government projects. But why anybody would go to all that trouble to find out what a historian knows—it beats me."

"That's a stumper, all right," Tracy admitted. "After all, the knowledge that Professor Mansard has is available in books. All a person would have to do would be to— That's it!"

"What's it?"

"Professor Mansard has spent a lifetime acquiring his knowledge. Almost everything that is known about man's history is stored away in his mind. If someone else wanted that knowledge, it would take him a lifetime, too, to get it—that is, if he had to read all the books. But suppose he was in a hurry. What do we do when we need a lot of information fast?"

Sam pointed. "The computer."

"Exactly. So, think of Professor Mansard as a computer. He has this great quantity of historical information stored in his mind. The quickest way for someone else to get that information would be to get it from the Professor's mind—doesn't that make sense,"

"I can't argue that," Sam replied. "But it still doesn't tell us why anybody would want the information."

Tracy sighed and sat back. "Science . . . history . . . science ... history ... what does it mean? There's a connection ... there's a key ... but what is it? Science ... what does that suggest to you, Sam?"

"Rockets? Outer-space?"

"Yes ... what else?"

"Stuff. Almost everything. Every day, science comes up with something new."

"Yes, this is the scientific— The Scientific Age! This is the Scientific Age, Sam! Today, the present. And what's the opposite of the present?"

"Yesterday."

"The Past. That's the connection, Sam! The Past and the Present. Science represents the Present, and history represents the Past. Between them, Dr. Zgani and Professor Mansard are in possession of almost the entire knowledge of the Present and the Past!"

"So?"

"Sam, if one person had all that knowledge, and if that one person knew how to use it—can you imagine what could happen?"

"Well . . . a lot, I guess."

"Yes, a great deal. Something good, perhaps. Or something very bad."

"Tracy, are you trying to tell me that there's somebody running around loose who knows everything that Dr. Zgani and Professor Mansard know?"

"I'm guessing, Sam."

"Okay, say you're right. *How* will he use it?"

"I don't know. And, at this point, perhaps he doesn't know either. Having the knowledge is one thing. Putting it to use is another. That, too, takes a specialized skill."

"I don't see what you're getting at," Sam said, puzzled.

Tracy picked up the tape from the computer. "Does this help? Remember what the computer told us?"

"Sure . . . Administrator. So?"

"Sam, what does an Administrator do? He puts knowledge and skills to use to accomplish a specific goal. Isn't it possible that whoever acquired the knowledge of the Present and the knowledge of the Past from Dr. Zgani and Professor Mansard now needs the knowledge of an Administrator to put it to use?"

Sam put his hands to his head. "If you say so, Tracy. I'm having a little trouble keeping up with you."

"If my theory is right," Tracy continued, "it will be

one of the country's top executives—some famous administrator—who will disappear next."

"Well, that makes it easy for us," Sam said. "All we have to do is put a watch on every executive in the country."

"Not all of them. Only the best-known. In fact, only the more famous ones who are right here in this city. This is where whoever is doing this is working. Let's get a list, Sam. A list of every well-known administrator in this part of the country. Then we'll just have to put as many of them as we can under surveillance."

Sam headed for the door. "There must be an Executives Club or something like that where I could get a list," he said. "I'll get right on it."

"Sam—"

"Yeah?"

"When you get the list, there's one name you can skip. Alex Halderman. I'm going to shadow him myself."

"I know that name," Sam frowned. "He's . . . what? Head of some foundation?"

"President of the Doremus Foundation," Tracy nodded. "He's, by far, the most famous administrator in this area. If I were whoever it is who's doing this, he's the man I'd pick. And, I know Halderman by sight, so it will be easy for me to keep a tail on him."

"Okay—luck."

Soon after Sam departed, Tracy left too. He got into his car and drove to the headquarters of the Doremus Foundation. It was a huge, old, stone-faced building near the center of the city. He parked, then walked to the entrance to the building. He waited until he saw a man exit. Then, started to enter, he suddenly stopped and spoke to the doorman.

"Wasn't that Mr. Halderman who just left?" Tracy said.

The doorman shook his head. "That don't even look nothing like Mr. Halderman," he replied. "Besides, Mr. Halderman's near always the last one to leave every night. You won't see him taking off from work in the middle of the day."

"My mistake," Tracy shrugged.

He entered the building. He had learned what he wanted to know—that Alex Halderman had not yet left for the day—but he did not want to create suspicion by immediately turning around and leaving after having asked the question. So, he walked up and down a few corridors, killing time, before he exited and returned to his car.

Tracy had a long wait. The hours slogged by. The only break in the monotony was when he received reports from headquarters on the radio. He was told that the search for the man with the black eye patch—Dutch Borgman—was proving fruitless; he had not been seen anywhere near his old haunts for over a year. Then Sam reported that he had obtained a list of the well-known executives in the area and that the top ten were being watched.

Then, at a little after ten-thirty that night, Tracy saw Alex Halderman leave the building. He was a middle-aged man, meticulously dressed, and carrying an attache case. After coming out the entrance, he walked toward the rear of the building, where the parking lot was located. A few minutes later, he reappeared, behind the wheel of a long, black Cadillac.

Tracy started his engine and followed the car. They drove through the city, almost to the outskirts. Then

Alex Halderman steered his car down into the subsurface garage of a luxury apartment building.

Tracy assumed that this was where Halderman lived, and that he would reach his apartment from inside, so that he would not appear again until morning. Thus, there was no point in Tracy losing a night's sleep. He radioed headquarters and asked for an officer who had night duty to be sent to take over the stake-out for him.

A few seconds after he had completed the call to headquarters, however, Tracy was surprised to see Halderman suddenly reappear. And he was not alone. He had emerged from the entrance to the garage. And he was accompanied by two men, one on either side of him. Tracy stared into the dimness—the man at Halderman's right was wearing a black eye patch!

Quickly, Tracy opened the door of his car. He started to jump out—then he hesitated. It looked as if Halderman were accompanying the two men willingly. They were walking toward a car that was parked on the street. The men were not holding Halderman, and they did not seem to be threatening him with a gun.

It occurred to Tracy that Halderman might be an accomplice of the two men rather than their victim. He eased back into the car and quietly closed the door and then continued to observe. If Halderman were somehow mixed up in what was happening—the abduction of Dr. Zgani and Professor Mansard—then it would be a mistake for Tracy to show his hand at this point. He would be wiser to follow Halderman and the two men and try to find out what they were up to.

The three got into the car. The man with the eye

patch got behind the wheel, Halderman sat in the front seat beside him, and the third man got into the rear seat. The car moved away from the curb. After a few seconds, Tracy pulled out and followed.

The car headed back toward the center of the city. Then when it reached there it made a left turn and once more headed for the outskirts. Tracy wondered if the men in the car knew that they were being followed. But they did not seem to be trying to lose him. Perhaps this was only a precaution—maybe they were keeping a lookout for a tail, but had not yet spotted him.

The car reached the edge of the city, then made a U-turn and started back in the direction from which it had just come. Puzzled, all Tracy could do was keep after the car and hope that the men were not aware of him. He doubted that they were, since they had made no attempt to elude him.

The car returned to the business section, then turned off into an area of old warehouses. There were very few other cars around, and even fewer pedestrians. Since there were no other obstacles between him and the car he was tailing, Tracy was able to drop back a bit and still keep it in sight. A few moments later he saw it pull over to the curb and stop. He did exactly the same thing.

The three men got out of the car and entered a building. Halderman still seemed to be accompanying them of his own free choice. Tracy got out of his own car and—moving at a leisurely pace—walked toward the building. When he reached the entrance, he glanced at it—and saw a wooden, windowless door—but did not stop. He moved on to the corner, crossed to the other side of the street, and then walked back in the direction of the building. When he was across from it he stopped and stood in the shadows.

There was a light on. It seemed to be on the second floor. Tracy pondered. What should he do? Call headquarters and have a squad of men sent out and break into the building? Or try to enter by himself and attempt to find out what was going on? As matters stood, he had no evidence of any wrong doing. All he had was a hunch. In fact, two hunches. One that the two men had abducted Halderman. And the other that the men had *not* abducted Halderman—that Halderman was involved with them in whatever it was they were doing.

He decided finally to make a preliminary investigation on his own. Leaving the shadows and crossing the street, he approached the doorway. When he reached it, he tried the knob. It turned. Slowly, he pushed open the door. There was a dim light inside. He could see a stairway that led upward. Then suddenly a face appeared in front of him—the face of a man with a black patch over his right eye. At the same instant there was a glint of light. Then Tracy was shoved. He found himself back on the street. The door slammed shut.

Tracy threw his weight against the door. But it held. He backed off and crashed against it once more. But, flimsy as it looked, it withstood the force. He decided he was wasting time trying to batter it down. There was no way of knowing what might be happening to Halderman—or, to put it another way, what Halderman might be doing—beyond the door. Quickly, he raced back along the street toward his car.

He reached the corner—and stopped! Where was his car? He should have reached it before he came to the corner. But it was nowhere in sight! How could that happen? He hadn't heard anything, he hadn't seen anything! How could a car, weighing several tons, simply vanish? Impossible!

Three

THERE WAS no time to waste asking himself questions. Tracy sprinted down the street until he reached a police call box. A few moments later he was in contact with the Chief, who shouted,

"Tracy! What happened? Where have you been? We've been scouring the town for you!"

"What are you talking about?" Tracy was puzzled. "I contacted you about an hour ago. Don't you remember? I called to ask you to send an officer to relieve me on the stake-out at Alex Halderman's apartment house."

"Tracy, it's happened to you too!" The Chief said excitedly. "You've been missing since last night—about twenty-four hours. Can't you remember?"

"Chief, is that supposed to be a joke? Are you serious?

"I swear it, Tracy. We found your car. But there was no trace of you anywhere. Can't you remember anything about it? Where are you now?"

Suddenly Tracy no longer doubted that he had been missing. He did not understand it, but he could not deny it. He told the Chief where he was calling from and asked him to hurry a squad of men to him to help break into the building where Alex Halderman and the two others had vanished.

It was not long before two squad cars pulled up at the call box. The Chief and Sam were in one car, accompanying the men. Tracy got into the lead car, and they drove to the building. When they reached it, they piled out of the cars, and Tracy ordered two of the officers to break down the door. One of them, curious, turned the knob. The door swung open.

Tracy stared at the open door, perplexed. "But only a few minutes ago it was locked. I tried to break it down."

"Tracy—only a few minutes ago, plus twenty-four hours," Sam said. "Don't you believe us?"

Tracy groaned. "Of course. It's just very difficult to realize. I understand now how Dr. Zgani and Professor Mansard felt. But that explains it. A lot has probably happened in that twenty-four hours."

"What did you think was in there?" the Chief asked.

"Alex Halderman. Two men picked him up. They brought him here. Or maybe he accompanied them willingly. I'm not sure. But, anyway, they came here, with Halderman and entered this building. I tried to follow. The door was open. I entered the building. Then I saw the fellow with the eye patch. Him . . . and a flash of light . . . something. Then the door slammed shut. I couldn't break it down. I headed back toward my car. But it was gone. So I found that call box and contacted you. It all happened so quickly. And yet . . . yet, somewhere, I lost twenty-four hours."

"Well, we can figure that out later," the Chief said. "Let's check this building."

Cautiously, they entered. The entranceway was dark, and cluttered with boxes and debris. No lights were on. An officer shined his flashlight beam up the stairs. A cat fled for cover.

"I've been in this building," Sam said. "I searched it earlier today."

"Why?" Tracy asked, puzzled.

"When we found your car up the street, we searched all the buildings in this area," Sam replied. "This one is a warehouse—or, used to be. It isn't used any more. It's going to be torn down."

"And you didn't find anything? Not *any*thing suspicious?"

Sam shook his head.

"I want to look anyway," Tracy said.

They proceeded up the steps. The second floor was littered with remnants of wooden crates. In the front there were two small offices, but there was no evidence that they had been occupied recently.

"Well, Tracy?" the Chief said.

"Those two men and Halderman came in here," Tracy replied stubbornly. "I'm sure of it."

"I don't doubt it," the Chief replied. "Alex Halderman is missing. We got a call early this morning from his wife. He didn't reach his apartment last night. We weren't too surprised—since we'd had the call from you that you'd followed him. Then we couldn't get in contact with you."

"What about him—have there been any further reports?" Tracy asked.

"None. He's still gone."

They left the building and got back into the squad cars and headed back toward headquarters.

"Apparently Halderman was abducted," Tracy said. "I wasn't sure. But he wasn't fighting it: that was what fooled me. How did they do it? How did they get him to go with them?"

"What happened to your twenty-four hours, that's what I'd like to know," Sam said.

Tracy sighed. "So would I, Sam . . . so would I."

At that moment, a call came in over the radio for the Chief. Alex Halderman had reappeared! Halderman had arrived at his apartment, completely unaware that he had been missing.

"I want to talk to him," Tracy said.

When they all returned to headquarters, Tracy and Sam got Tracy's car and drove to Alex Halderman's apartment building. They found a uniformed officer standing guard at the Halderman's apartment door. He let them in, and they were met by Mrs. Halderman. She escorted them to a small study, where Alex Halderman was working at a desk.

By then, Alex Halderman had realized that he had lost twenty-four hours out of his life. But he was at a loss to explain the mystery to Tracy.

"I feel fine," he said to Tracy and Sam. "I'm willing to believe that it happened, but there's nothing that I can tell you about it."

"The man with the black eye patch, do you remember him?" Tracy asked.

Halderman looked at him blankly.

Tracy then explained that he had followed Halderman when he had left his office and had seen him depart—apparently willingly—with the two men. He explained to Halderman why he had been following him: his idea about the disappearances.

"Well . . . your theory seems to make sense—the scientist, the historian and the administrator," Halderman replied. "But I have no recollection—none whatsoever—of leaving the garage with those two men. As far as I remember, I left my office, I drove to the apartment building, I parked my car in the garage, then I got into the elevator and came here to my apartment. That's when I discovered that I'd been missing."

Tracy and Sam questioned Halderman a while longer, then left. He had given them no new clues.

As they drove back toward headquarters, Tracy said, "Well, if my theory is right, whoever is doing this has everything he needs now. He has the knowledge of the Past, and the knowledge of the Present, and, with the knowledge of the Administrator, he knows how to use them."

"It's still a guess, Tracy," Sam reminded him.

"Yes, that's true."

"The man with the eye patch you saw—was it Dutch Borgman? We still haven't found any trace of him."

"It may have been," Tracy replied. "Like Professor Mansard, I can't be absolutely sure. I got only a glimpse of him. And I was distracted by that sudden flash of light." He scowled darkly. "That flash of light . . . could that be the key?"

"Were you hypnotized, maybe?" Sam suggested.

"Possibly. It was a state of unawareness. But real hypnotism . . . no, I doubt it. Something else. Let's assume that this person wanted to get information from the three men he had abducted. A man under a hypnotic spell won't cooperate unless he wants to. And I doubt that any of the three would give up their knowledge willingly." He shook his head. "No, I don't think it was hypnotism."

"Some kind of instant brain-washing?" Sam said.

"Mmmmm . . . that might be closer to it. But with no after-effect. None of us feel anything, not Zgani, not Mansard, not Halderman, not me."

"I wonder why it was done to you?" Sam said.

"Yes, that's puzzling. Unless it was simply because I was a threat. I was trying to get into the building. Presumably there was something in there that somebody didn't want me to see. But what? What was in that building? You searched it, and you found nothing."

"Whatever it was could have been removed by the time I got there," Sam pointed out. "Or, maybe it was just Halderman they didn't want you to see—or find."

"Possibly. Sam . . . I'm trying to remember . . . there was a dim bulb on in the entranceway. That flash of light could have been that bulb flashing on something shiny . . . something metal. Maybe a hypodermic syringe—a needle. That might explain it. A drug. I might have been given an injection."

Sam nodded. "I'll buy that."

"Let's say that it happened this way: I opened that door. The guy with the eye patch was waiting for me. He stuck me with his needle, and I immediately entered the state of unawareness. Completely out. I was taken somewhere. Probably along with Halderman. We were kept there, probably until just before the drug would wear off, and then we were returned. I was taken back to that warehouse, and shoved out the door, and the door was slammed in my face. Twenty-four hours had passed, but I didn't know it."

"It sounds loony, but I suppose it's possible," Sam replied. "It would fit the other disappearances too. Remember?"

"Of course. Dr. Zgani when he stopped to open the gate to his property. And Professor Mansard when he reached the University parking lot and started to get out of his car—he recalled seeing the man with the eye patch. And Alex Halderman when he drove his car into the apartment house garage."

"Well, now—maybe—we know *how* it was done. But why?" Sam said.

"For the knowledge that those three men have—I still think it's that," Tracy replied.

"Okay, say you're right. Where does that put us?"

"A couple steps closer," Tracy replied. "But to what, I'm not sure."

They had reached headquarters, and they went to the Chief's office, and they told him what they had found out from Alex Halderman, which was next to nothing. Then Tracy explained the further development of his theory to the Chief.

"It sounds like science fiction," the Chief replied.

"I agree," Tracy said. "Yet, I have the feeling that it's based in fact. There was an experiment like that recently. Something that I read about or saw. I just can't remember."

"Something that explains this?" Sam said.

Tracy nodded. "It's on the tip of my mind."

"Well, work on it," the Chief said. "Maybe it will come to you. Right now, I think we could all use a little sleep. Especially you, Tracy."

The following morning, Tracy returned alone to the warehouse district. He walked slowly through the area, talking to the workmen—the truckers, the loaders, the laborers—asking if anyone had noticed the man with the black eye patch in the neighborhood. A few said they had. One man remembered seeing him enter the abandoned building into which Tracy had watched him disappear with Alex Halderman. But no one knew who he was. Or if they did, they would not admit it to Tracy.

Back at headquarters he found a report on Dutch Borgman on his desk. Borgman, it seemed had recently spent some time in Europe, and he was thought to have returned. But there was no further trace of him. Tracy sent the report to Sam, then, once more, concentrated on trying to recall what he had heard about that might explain the mysterious disappearances.

A few minutes later he received a telephone call. There was a muffled voice at the other end of the line. The caller refused to identify himself. He asked if Tracy were the cop who had been seeking information about Dutch Borgman in the warehouse district. "Yes!" Tracy said, excitedly. The caller told him that Borgman could be found at a certain address. Then he hung up.

The call gave Tracy information he had not had before. When he was asking questions in the warehouse district he had not mentioned Borgman's name. But the caller had used the name. It was an indication that Dutch Borgman and the man with the black eye patch were the same man.

Tracy immediately hurried to the address he had been given. It was in a rundown area of the city. At first he could not find the exact number: it was not posted on any building. But he finally decided that it was the address of a small, dilapidated hotel. He entered the dingy lobby, which seemed to be deserted. Finally, however, near the rear, he spotted the desk. There was a young woman behind it. She was fairly attractive, in a coarse way, and did not appear to belong in the setting.

"I'm looking for a man named Borgman," Tracy said to her.

"Room 208," she replied, lowering her eyes.

"Does he live here, or is he just stopping here?"

The woman shrugged, refusing to face Tracy directly. "Ask him," she replied.

The stairway was located around the corner from the desk. It was dimly lit by a naked light bulb at the second floor landing. Tracy proceeded upward cautiously, bothered by the desk clerk's evasive manner, suspecting that finding Dutch Borgman was not going to be as easy as this.

When he reached the second floor he began checking the door numbers. Number 208 was the fourth door down from the landing. Tracy stood back from it, then, reaching out, knocked.

There was no response from inside.

He called out. "Borgman?"

Still, no sound.

Tracy rapped on the door once more, and called out again.

Silence.

Remaining to the side of the doorway, Tracy reached for the knob, found it, and turned it. The door was not locked. He thought for a moment, still suspicious. Then, still standing clear of the doorway, he gave the door a shove. As it swung open, a shot rang out. Tracy jumped back. A bullet lodged in the wall directly across from the doorway.

Tracy whipped out his pistol and waited. But there was no further sound from inside the room. He jumped in front of the opening, his gun ready. It was a small room and he could see almost the entire interior. It did not appear to be occupied.

Warily, Tracy stepped into the room. There was a bed—undisturbed—and a rickety chest of drawers. The floor was rugless. Paint was peeling from the walls. Here and there the plaster was cracked. There was a chair facing the doorway, and attached to it was a .44 pistol. A cord was fixed to the trigger of the gun, then run through a small pulley and tied to the doorknob. If Tracy had been standing in the doorway when he opened the door he would now most likely be dead.

He unfastened the gun from the chair, then wrapped it in a handkerchief and stuffed it into his pocket. After that, he searched the room thoroughly, but he found nothing more of any interest. So, he left the room and headed back down the stairs.

The woman was no longer behind the desk.

He called out. "Hello! Where are you!"

He heard a rattling noise. But no one appeared. The woman, evidently, had been stationed at the desk for the single purpose of steering him toward the trap. But what had happened to her?

He heard the rattling noise again. It seemed to be coming from somewhere behind the desk. And then he saw a door. It appeared to be a door to a small closet, located a few feet behind the counter.

Tracy circled the desk and opened the door. There was an elderly man inside the closet. He was bound and gagged. He had been kicking at the door, causing the sound that Tracy had heard.

Tracy quickly untied him.

"Who're you!" the old man demanded.

Tracy identified himself. "What happened to you?" he asked.

"Them two!" he replied indignantly. "I was right there at the desk, and they come in. Then that one with the dingus over his eye, he hit me. Pow! The next thing I knowed, here I was, in here, all roped up. Did you get 'em?"

Tracy shook his head. "What do you mean, a 'dingus?' An eye patch?"

"Right. Over his eye—a black dingus. Him and that woman."

"Had you ever seen him before?"

"Nope. What was it all about?"

"Does the name Carl Borgman, or Dutch Borgman, mean anything to you?"

"Not a blasted thing. Did they rob me?"

"I wouldn't know."

The old man opened a drawer behind the desk. There were a few wrinkled bills and some change in it. "All there," he said. "How do you figure that? Didn't take a penny."

"Maybe it was a practical joke," Tracy smiled. "Are you all right?"

"Sure—I guess so. Kind of sore back there on the head where he konked me."

"I'll send an officer around," Tracy said. "Give him a full report."

"Yeah . . . well, all right."

Tracy left the hotel and got back into his car. He radioed in to report the skirmish and to have headquarters send the man on the beat to the hotel to make out further report on the assault on the old man. Then he drove back toward headquarters.

Sam and the Chief were waiting for him.

"I picked up your call on the radio," Sam explained. "What's it all about?"

Tracy told them exactly what had happened.

"Somebody is getting nervous," he said. "I'm positive now that Dutch Borgman is mixed up in this. Somebody got to him and told him that I was asking questions in the warehouse district about a man with an eye patch. He figured that I'd identified him—that I knew exactly who I was looking for."

"So he set up that trap at the hotel to put you out of the way," Sam said.

"That's the way it looks."

"I don't know," the Chief said doubtfully. "This isn't Borgman's kind of job. He's a strongarm man. He's done time for robbery and assault. But kidnapping scientists and historians and executives . . . it's just not Borgman's racket."

"I suspect he's *still* doing strongarm work," Tracy said. "He's not the top man in this—I'd bet on that. We're looking for someone with brains, not brawn. But if we can find the man with brawn—Borgman—he may lead us to the man with brains."

"How brainy could he be?" Sam said. "The way he tried to trap you wasn't too smart."

"It wasn't so bad," Tracy replied. "It was pretty well set up. If that woman hadn't made me suspicious, I might have walked in through that doorway and got a slug in me."

"Now that—that isn't Borgman's way of operating either," the Chief said. "If he wanted to kill a man, he'd face him and gun him down."

"Exactly," Tracy nodded. "But this was very carefully thought out—and in a short space of time. It wasn't long after I returned from the warehouse district before I got that call, telling me I could find Borgman at that address. The man we're looking for thinks, and he thinks fast. He covered every angle—as far as we know. There was nothing in that room that could be traced. Except the pistol. I dropped it off at the lab to have it gone over for fingerprints or some kind of identification, but I'd bet money that we won't find anything on it."

The Chief's phone rang. He answered it, listened a moment, then handed it to Tracy. "For you."

"Yes—Tracy here," Tracy said into the receiver. Then he smiled, nodding. "Yes, Professor, of course I remember you. How could I possibly forget?"

He was on the phone a few more minutes, listening mostly, then he hung up.

"Professor Mansard?" Sam guessed.

"He has something he wants to tell me," Tracy replied. "He's on his way over here. It's something about his memory. It seems to be acting up on him."

Sam laughed. "The absent-minded professor."

"That may be it," Tracy replied. "But he—"

The phone rang again. This time, Tracy, who was near it, picked it up. It was a lab technician calling, reporting on the examination of the pistol that Tracy had brought in. After a moment, Tracy hung up again.

"I was right," he said to the Chief and Sam. "Nothing. No fingerprints. The serial numbers have been filed down. There's no way of tracing it."

"That makes you right on both counts," the Chief said. "The man we want is a thinker, all right—and a fast thinker."

"I wouldn't be surprised to find out that we're up against a computer," Sam said. "How about it, Tracy? How do you get along with that computer we have here at headquarters? Maybe it's tired of answering your questions. Maybe it hired Dutch Borgman to get rid of you."

"I'll go ask it," Tracy smiled.

There was a knock at the door.

"Yes?" the Chief called.

The door opened and an officer put his head in. "A Professor Mansard is here to see Tracy," he said.

"Coming," Tracy replied.

The door closed.

"Shall I have the professor come in here, Chief? Do you want to hear this?" Tracy said.

The Chief shook his head. "Too busy. This isn't the only case the Department has, you know. Tell me about it later—if it's worth telling."

Tracy and Sam left the Chief's office and walked toward the reception area.

"Have you remembered yet what you were trying to remember?" Sam said.

"What?"

"You said something about an experiment or something that might explain these disappearances."

"Oh . . . that. No. It had something to do with the mind . . . an experiment on the mind. Something of that nature. I read about it, I think, in one of the scientific publications. Tonight, I'll go through my files. Maybe I'll come across it."

"And speaking of minds . . ." Sam said, gesturing ahead.

Tracy looked and saw Professor Mansard standing in the doorway of the reception area. He looked quite troubled.

Four

TRACY, SAM and Professor Mansard went to one of the interrogation rooms, where they could have privacy. The Professor was nervous. As they sat around the table he drummed his fingers on the table top, scowling concernedly.

"What's the problem?" Tracy asked.

"This is a little difficult for me to say," the Professor replied. "Whenever a teacher . . . one of us ivory tower people ... has trouble with his memory, the inclination is always to dismiss it with some comment like ... well, absent-minded professor ..."

Tracy glanced at Sam. And Sam looked sheepish.

"It's expected of us, that—with our heads in the clouds—we'll be forgetful," Professor Mansard continued. "But, believe me, I'm not normally that way at all. Especially when it comes to my subject—history."

"What's happened?" Tracy asked.

"I'm afraid this is going to sound very unimportant to you."

"Let me be the judge of that."

"Well," Professor Mansard sighed, "I first became aware of it yesterday afternoon. I was lecturing to some students—graduate students—and I was discussing the Prague Conference of 1813, when I suddenly found myself rattling on about the London Proclamation of 1908. I was stunned when I discovered it."

Tracy and Sam waited for him to say more.

"Don't you see?" he said. "Besides coming almost a

century apart, the two acts have absolutely nothing in common. And yet to me there seemed to be a parallel. I was discussing them almost as if they were one and the same."

"Yeah . . . so?" Sam said.

"My mind is compartmentalized," Professor Mansard explained. "But one compartment had, somehow, slopped over into another compartment. Surely, you understand."

Sam shook his head. "Maybe it was just a slip of the tongue."

"No, no. I actually thought that the Conference and the Proclamation were comparable. I had them muddled. It was my students' questions that caught me up. I had to go back to the books and re-learn the facts."

"Has this happened in any other instance?" Tracy asked.

"Not yet. At least, not that I know of." He shuddered. "But it's frightening. I'm not sure I can trust my knowledge."

"Is there any way to explain it?" Tracy wondered.

"I really don't know. But it has occurred to me that something might have happened to my memory during the twenty-four hour period when I was missing. That's why I thought I'd best mention it to you. I was hoping . . . well, I was hoping that you might provide an explanation."

Tracy shook his head. "I'm afraid I can't. Not yet."

Professor Mansard sighed again. "It's very disturbing. I have no way of knowing what other facts in my mind may be jumbled about. This could completely destroy my effectiveness as a teacher. I can even see myself having to go back and re-educate myself—completely."

"I hope it won't come to that," Tracy said sympathetically. "Has anything else happened? Have you felt ill in any way? Has there been any loss of memory in other ways—other than your work, that is?"

Professor Mansard shook his head. "Only this one instance."

"Well, then, I wouldn't worry too much about it."

The Professor rose. "I thought it might give you a clue to the meaning of this ridiculous business. You'll keep what I've told you in confidence, I assume. If it got out, of course, I can imagine what they might think about it at the University. 'Old Mansard is cracking up,' they'd say."

"I won't say a word," Tracy assured him. "I'm sure there's no reason to."

"Well . . ." He shrugged. "Baffling . . . baffling, to say the very least."

Tracy and Sam walked with the Professor to the exit. When he had gone, they returned to the interrogation room, where they could have quiet.

"That was a waste of time," Sam commented.

"Maybe not. On the surface, I know, what he told us doesn't seem especially important—or even to make much sense. But when you think about it a little more, and when you consider the motive—"

"Whose motive?" Sam asked puzzledly.

"The motive of whoever kidnapped the Professor, Dr. Zgani and Alex Halderman."

"I didn't know we'd established that," Sam said.

"All right—my *guess* at what the motive is, then. My guess that the purpose was to acquire the knowledge of a famous scientist, historian and administrator. If you consider that, then what Professor Mansard just told us fits in very neatly."

"Would you mind explaining it to me?" Sam said dourly.

"Suppose the knowledge was removed from the three men's minds. Then, suppose—"

"Hold it," Sam interrupted. "Removed how?"

"I don't know. I'm just supposing. Supposing the knowledge was removed, and then assume that it was put back in. But, assume further that, in Professor Mansard's case, the knowledge was put back in incorrectly."

"Tracy, you're getting too far out for me," Sam said. "I just don't follow it."

"Well, I'm only suggesting a possibility," Tracy said. "I admit—" He suddenly sat up straight. "That's it! Of course. Now, I remember!"

"Good," Sam said glumly. "What?"

"That experiment! Remember? I mentioned it to you. I couldn't remember the details—or where I'd read about it or heard about it. Now, I recall. It was in an issue of a scientific magazine." He got to his feet. "I'm sure I still have the copy."

Tracy hurried from the room. Sam tagged after him, at a more moderate pace, and then caught up with him a few seconds later at his desk. Tracy was going through a bottom drawer, looking at the dates on a collection of scientific journals. At last, he found the issue he was searching for. Then, while Sam waited patiently, he settled back in his chair and began reading an article.

After a while, Tracy put the magazine down. "This may be it," he said. "This article is about an experiment being conducted by a scientist named Gustave Moehler. He's produced a drug—he calls it a mind-emptying drug. And, if what he claims is true, it could be a drug that was used on our three kidnapped men—and me."

"What exactly does he claim?"

"The drug, according to Moehler, when injected into the blood stream, puts the subject into a trance. He's completely unaware of everything around him and everything that's happening to him. And—listen to this—the effect of the drug lasts for *exactly twenty-four hours.* Not twenty-three hours and fifty minutes, or twenty-four hours and ten minutes, but *exactly* twenty-four hours. That's a feature of it that Moehler hasn't been able to explain—but he reported it."

"Is that all it does?" Sam asked.

"No. While the subject is in this trance, his mind can be completely emptied. Everything, every thought, can be removed. It's very simple. Whoever administers the drug merely asks the subject to tell him everything he knows—and the subject does."

"I know a lot of people who will do that without a drug," Sam said. "But what I don't understand is why anybody would *want* to know everything that somebody else knows."

"Moehler's idea is to use it to cure insanity. He would have the subject empty his mind completely, and he would put all of his thoughts on tape. Next, those thoughts that were the basis for the insanity would be erased—snipped out of the tape. The remaining thoughts would then be played back to the subject—he would re-absorb them."

"Hey! That sounds like a good idea," Sam said, finally impressed.

"Or a bad idea—if the wrong person got hold of the drug," Tracy said.

"Do you think that's what's happened?"

"I can't be sure. But it's possible."

"It would explain what happened to Professor Mansard's memory," Sam said. "Somebody could have injected him with the drug, then put all his knowledge on tape, then, when he was putting it back in, goofed. A faulty tape or something—is that possible?"

"Very possible," Tracy nodded.

"Wait a minute, though, Tracy," Sam frowned. "Let's say that this somebody has all this knowledge on tape—the scientist's and the historian's and the administrator's—what's he going to do with it? How can he use it? It might be interesting to listen to, but of what practical use would it be?"

"I can't answer that," Tracy replied. "But, if we locate whoever it is, I imagine we'll find out."

"Yeah . . . well, there's a needle-in-a-haystack assignment for you—locate him where?"

"It says here in the article that Moehler is still experimenting with the drug—that he doesn't feel that it's ready for general use yet. It just may be that Gustave Moehler himself is the man we want. If he's still experimenting, he may have been using our scientist and our historian and our administrator as guinea pigs."

"That's illegal."

"Illegal and immoral. I think we'd better find Gustave Moehler—and fast."

Tracy telephoned Dr. Zgani. Zgani was acquainted with Moehler, and told Tracy where he could find him.

"He has a laboratory up in the hills," Tracy reported to Sam after he had ended the conversation. "He lives up there too. According to Dr. Zgani, he's a crusty old fellow, he doesn't care to have people around, he works alone. Let's drive up there and—"

Tracy's phone rang.

It was the Chief calling. He wanted Sam for another assignment.

"I'll go talk to Moehler alone," Tracy said.

"Just don't let him get anywhere near you with a needle," Sam warned.

Tracy left headquarters and drove out of the city. Following Dr. Zgani's directions, he headed up into the mountainous area surrounding the town. The road he took wound in and out between the hills, rising steeply. He reached a section where the road had been cut out of the side of a mountain. To his right was a sheer drop of over a thousand feet. He drove slowly and cautiously.

He had no trouble finding Gustave Moehler's laboratory. It was a small cement-block building, tucked in between two rises, not far from the road. There was an old car parked behind it—Moehler's, Tracy guessed.

The place seemed closed. No sign of life was in evidence. And when Tracy knocked on the door he got no reply. He tried the knob, but the door was locked.

"Moehler!"

There was no answer.

He circled the building, trying all the windows: they were locked too.

Finally, Tracy walked to the old car and opened the door on the driver's side. At that instant he heard a sound behind him. He whipped around, just in time to catch a glimpse of a man who was wearing a black eye patch. Then he felt a sudden sharp pain at the back of his head, and he lost consciousness.

Tracy was in darkness, being bumped about. There was a blindfold over his eyes. His wrists were manacled. He realized he was inside something and fortunately his arms were locked in front, so he could feel around, trying to figure out where he was. His fingers touched something made of metal. But that was no help.

The bumping and movement puzzled him. He was definitely inside something that was rolling, or was— A car! He was in the trunk of a car. He stretched, feeling around again. He was in the trunk of a car. But whose car, and going where?

He hadn't been injected with the drug, he decided. He was completely aware of what was happening. Unless, of course, this was twenty-four hours later and the effect of the drug had just worn off. But the back of his head was still sore. Most likely only minutes had passed since he had been struck from behind.

Tracy listened intently, hoping to get some clue to where the car was from the sounds outside the trunk. He heard other cars, rushing by, and somewhere, very faintly, a fire siren. Evidently he was back in the city.

As the car continued on its way the ride became smoother; Tracy was no longer being bounced about. The tires were producing a different sound, as if the car were passing over iron grillwork. What could that mean? A bridge? Yes. But which bridge? There were so many in the city.

He heard the hollow, harsh voice of a sound truck. It was announcing the coming of the circus. Quickly, Tracy smashed his wristwatch against the floor. Then he touched the dial. Yes, the crystal had broken and his fingers found the hands. He estimated the time at a little after two o'clock. Later, by finding out where the sound truck had been at that time, he could estimate where he had been too. The information might be useful.

The car suddenly stopped. He heard two doors being slammed. Then he heard the trunk being opened. A little light filtered in under the blindfold. But not enough—he was still in the dark. Hands grasped him. He was dragged roughly from the trunk and put on his feet. The trunk door slammed closed. Then Tracy was pushed and guided along. Once more, he touched the watch face, checking the hands for the time.

From the feeling underfoot, Tracy guessed he was walking on cement. Then all at once he tripped and fell forward. There was laughter—two men laughing. He was against a stairway.

"Up!" a gravelly voice prodded him.

He was dragged to his feet. Then he was marched up a flight of steps. A few seconds after he reached the level, he was shoved. He lost his balance and fell forward, landing on his chest and face.

Hands got hold of him again. He was rolled over. The blindfold was removed. The man with the black eye patch—it was Dutch Borgman; now Tracy was certain of his identity—was grinning down at him. The other man, smaller and with a weasel-like face, was standing a few paces away. They were in a small room. It had no furniture, there was no floor covering, and the one window was painted over and covered with heavy steel mesh.

"How'dja like the ride, Tracy?" Borgman snarled. "We took the scenic route—but maybe you didn't notice."

Tracy studied him calmly. "What do you want with me, Borgman?"

"Me? I don't want nothin' with you. I don't want *no*

cop. But you I want less than any of them. If I had my way about it, I'd've popped you off out there at that lab."

"I guess you were disappointed when you missed popping me off at that hotel," Tracy said.

"I wouldn't've missed if I'd done it my way," Borgman growled. "It's usin' brains, tryin' to knock off a cop, that bugs it up."

"Yes, brains definitely isn't your way," Tracy said. "Who is supplying the brains?"

"When it's time for you to find out, you'll find out. Until then—keep quiet." He turned to his companion. "Hold your gun on him," he commanded.

The smaller man pulled out a pistol and pointed it at Tracy. Then Borgman bent down and removed the handcuffs from Tracy's wrists.

"Is that wise?" Tracy smiled.

"You ain't goin' nowhere," Borgman told him. "There's the window and the door. It'd take a bull-dozer to bust out that window. And you come out that door and you'll get a bellyful of lead. Check?"

"Check," Tracy nodded. "How long do you intend to keep me here?"

" 'Til Mr. Computer gives me the word I can bump you off."

"Mr. Who?"

"Don't ask, I told you."

"He—whoever he is—I take it, is the brains."

"You want a foot in your face, Tracy?"

"That isn't exactly what I was looking for when I started out this morning," Tracy smiled.

"Then shut—just shut."

Borgman and the other man left the room and Tracy heard a key turn in the lock of the door. He got to his feet and moved to the door and gently turned the knob, just to check. But the door was definitely locked. Next, he went to the window. He tested the strength of the steel mesh. Borgman, he decided, was right—a bulldozer would be needed to break through the window.

He began looking for some other way to escape. He rapped lightly on a wall, sounding it for thickness.

To his great surprise, he heard a voice speak his name in response to the knock.

Tracy put his ear to the wall. "Yes, this is Tracy," he said. "Who's there?"

The voice came through again. "You don't know me. I'm Gustave Moehler. I'm a prisoner too."

"I don't know you," Tracy said. "But I know about you. I was looking for you when Borgman and that other fellow caught me at your lab. Why are they holding you? Do they have your mind-emptying drug?"

"Yes! How do you know about it? They used it on you, I know. I was there—in the warehouse. They brought you and that other man in—I don't know who *he* was. But you shouldn't be able to remember that. You should have been completely unaware while you were under the influence of the drug.

"I was. It's too complicated to explain now," Tracy said. "Is this wall as thin as it seems? Can I break through to you?"

"You probably could," Moehler replied. "But there would be no point to it. There is no place to go. I'm in a room much like the one you are occupying."

"Can they hear us?" Tracy asked.

"I doubt it. This is a house. They stay in the kitchen. It is down the corridor. They watch the doors from there to make sure that we do not escape."

"Then can you tell me what this is all about?" Tracy said.

"No. I just don't know. I was in my laboratory and they came and they took me away. They forced me to give them my drug. They have been using it—using it on people. But I don't know why. I don't even know why they are keeping me here—they have my drug. I think they are going to kill me. I don't understand why they haven't done it already. It is all very much a mystery to me."

"Who is 'they'?" Tracy asked. "Borgman and the little guy and who else?"

"There are several of them. I do not know them all by name. I see them. They take me out of here to feed me—they take me to the kitchen. But, by 'who,' I suppose you mean Mr. Computer. He is their leader."

"Computer! Borgman used that name. Is it a name?"

"That is what he calls himself. That and his initials. He says he is I.B.M. Computer. It must be a fiction that he has dreamed up."

"Hasn't he told you anything?"

"Nothing. I have seen some things, and heard some things, but I have been told nothing. He must have some further use for me, but he has not said."

"How did you know my name?"

"I told you—I saw you at the warehouse. We were all at the warehouse before we came here. You were brought in—you and the other man. Mr. Computer was very disturbed. He decided that we all had to leave. We came here. And then, just before your twenty-four hour period was to end, you were taken away. I think you were taken back to the warehouse. I heard them talking."

Tracy asked, "Where is this Computer? Is he here?"

"I believe so. Somewhere in the house. But I am not positive."

"Is there anything in your room that I could use as a weapon?" Tracy asked.

"Nothing. It is bare."

"Then there isn't much I can do—for either of us," Tracy said. "We'll just have to wait, and see what happens."

"I wish I knew what Mr. Computer wants with us. How is he using my drug?"

"He's collecting knowledge," Tracy replied. "I'm pretty sure of that. But why, what he intends to do with it—that, I just can't figure out."

"Knowledge—I don't understand?"

Tracy explained to him that Mr. Computer had abducted Dr. Zgani, Professor Mansard and Alex Halderman and had, apparently, used the drug on them to get their specialized knowledge from them.

"I know Dr. Zgani," Moehler said. "I didn't see him here."

"Maybe they kept you in hiding."

"Yes, that's possible. But I wonder—" Then suddenly Tracy heard another voice on the other side of the wall—Borgman's. His words did not come through clearly, but Tracy could tell that he was angry. Following Borgman's abrupt appearance there was a sound of scuffling. And then silence.

Tracy waited a few seconds, listening. Then he called. "Moehler . . . ?"

There was no reply.

He guessed that Gustave Moehler had been taken away, or silenced. He hoped the scientist was still alive.

Tracy tried calling to him again. "Moehler . . . can you hear me?"

Nothing.

"Are you gagged? If you are—if you can move, kick on the wall."

But there was still no response.

Then he heard sounds in the corridor. He moved quickly to the door and put his ear to the keyhole, listening intently. Something was being dragged. A body? Moehler? Possibly. But then, possibly not. It was frustrating not to be able to see what was going on.

The sound moved away.

Tracy looked at his watch. It was early afternoon—still daylight. Daylight . . . and he had been brought to a house, manacled and blindfolded. How had they transferred him from the car to the house without running the risk of someone seeing him? Unless they parked the car inside the house. That might explain it—perhaps the house had an underground garage, or a garage that was part of the house. He remembered standing on cement—the garage floor, probably.

He moved to the window again. He locked his fingers in the mesh and pulled with all his strength. But the effort was a waste. Nothing gave.

A moment later, Tracy heard the door open behind him. He turned. In the doorway of his room an immense fat man was standing. He was dressed in a business suit that had quite obviously been cut especially to fit his gigantic proportions. His head was bald and seemed to be an almost perfect square. His eyes were bright and sparkling, like two small, flashing lights. He was smiling a tight, humorless smile.

"Good day, Mr. Tracy," he said crisply. "I am I.B.M. Computer!"

Five

TRACY OBSERVED Computer interestedly, offering no reply. He was fascinated. Computer seemed to him to be more like a machine than a man. But as he looked closer he saw that this was only an illusion. Without a doubt, Computer was human. He had human flesh. And his movements were human; smooth and perfectly coordinated.

"You are baffled, Mr. Tracy," Computer said. "You are baffled by me, and you are baffled by the situation." The tight, thin smile appeared on his face again. "Baffled, but not afraid. The unknown does not frighten you. I know your mind quite well, Mr. Tracy."

"That gives you a certain advantage," Tracy replied. "As you say, I'm baffled—I don't know your mind at all. Who are you? Or, should I ask 'what' are you?"

" 'Who' is correct," Computer replied. "I'm flesh and blood, the same as you, Mr. Tracy. More highly developed, but essentially the same." He tapped his skull. "It is the mind that makes the difference."

"Computer? Is that your actual name?"

"No. It's the name I have taken. It suits me so well. My brain, you see, functions in much the same way that a computer functions."

Tracy shook his head. "No, I don't see."

"I am a freak, Mr. Tracy. I am, I suspect, a model of what all men will be in some distant future. As I just explained, I have a computer mind. My brain is able to record everything I hear, and file it for later use. Everything I have ever learned can be recalled in an instant. Not only that, but my brain can also evaluate every bit of information that it has stored away."

Tracy peered at him skeptically.

"Ah . . . you find that difficult to believe. It is a shame that you will not live to realize that what I am telling you is the absolute truth. But, unfortunately, at the moment, you are a danger to me."

"Since you intend to kill me, there's no reason why you can't tell me what this is all about, is there?" Tracy said. "Dead, I'll have no way of using the information."

"That is quite correct."

"Dr. Zgani, Professor Mansard, Alex Halderman—you wanted their knowledge, is that right? That's why you kidnapped them."

"Correct again, Mr. Tracy. Everything that they know, I now know. The entire range of their knowledge is now filed away in my memory banks. I can recall it in a matter of a split instant."

"And the reason?"

"Isn't that obvious, Mr. Tracy? What is it that we all want? Control—absolute control—over our fellow human beings—isn't that it?"

"I hope not," Tracy replied.

"You are not being honest with yourself. You know that it's true. Every man wants to be the Supreme Power, Mr. Tracy. Many have tried. All have failed. They failed because they did not have the necessary knowledge of their fellow human beings to manipulate them perfectly. I, however, now have that knowledge."

Tracy sighed. "You're human, all right," he said.

"Oh, yes ... very human. But a superior human. And that is not an easy thing to be, Mr. Tracy. I have been a freak from the very beginning. As a child, my mind was superior not only to other children's, but also to adults. Can you imagine how I was treated? Adults were afraid of me. Even my own parents were frightened by my superior mind. It is a lonely thing to be feared, Mr. Tracy . . . a lonely, lonely thing."

Tracy nodded. "Yes, I can understand that."

"Then you can understand how natural it was for me to hate."

"Yes. And this plan of yours, I can understand that, too. Revenge? Is that it?"

"Call it that if you choose. Perhaps you are partly right. But I see it as something else ... something larger, greater. Things will be much different when I am in control of society. There will be no more cruelty. I will purify mankind. Those who have cruel thoughts will be destroyed."

Tracy smiled thinly. "You see no cruelty in that–in destroying?"

"No. It is only a necessary step."

"Just as killing me is a necessary step?"

"Correct. I am not yet ready to put my plan into effect. There are details yet that have to be worked out. And you were getting too close to understanding what I have in mind, Mr. Tracy. If my plan were known, society would rise against me. So I must make certain that it does not become known."

"So I must be removed. And what about Gustave Moehler?"

"He, too, was a danger."

"Is he dead?"

"Quite."

Tracy looked away. He wondered what chance he would have against Computer if he attacked him. Computer was a giant of a man, extremely heavy. Perhaps he was too heavy to be quick.

"This knowledge," Tracy said, stalling. "How exactly do you intend to use it?"

Computer smiled the brittle smile again. "I understand what you are attempting, Mr. Tracy. You hope to gain time. You hope to distract me, then attack me. It will not work."

"I'm interested, that's all," Tracy replied.

"Yes . . . I know." The smile vanished. "My plan is simple, really," Computer continued. "In my brain, there is now stored all of the vitally important knowledge of the Past and Present. The Past, of course, is the most necessary element. History, Mr. Tracy, is the record of how man thinks and functions. It isn't just events and dates. Oh, no, it is much, much more than that. For those events are the work of men."

"Yes, I understand that."

"History is full of mistakes, Mr. Tracy. Other men, as I said, have attempted to control the world, to gain supreme power over their fellow men. And, again as I mentioned before, they have failed. I now know why they failed. The record of history has revealed it to me. I will not make those same mistakes."

"Perhaps there are other mistakes—mistakes that men haven't yet made," Tracy said. "You may be the one to make them."

"There is little likelihood of that. I have also, as you well know, absorbed the knowledge of today's most renowned administrator—Mr. Halderman. Using his methods, I will put the knowledge of the historian and the scientist to work—and I will be invulnerable."

Tracy braced himself, preparing to fly at Computer.

"That is useless," Computer said. "Without a firearm, you are powerless against me, Mr. Tracy. Don't waste what little time you have plotting to attack me."

Tracy stared at him, surprised.

"I know everything that is going on in your mind," Computer said. "Are you forgetting? You were my prisoner for twenty-four hours. I emptied your mind. I took every particle of your knowledge and stored it in my memory banks. I am now able to think exactly as you think, Mr. Tracy. Thus, I can anticipate every move you make. I know perfectly what you are going to do before you do it. Because you are a thinking man, Mr. Tracy. You think before you act. It is natural to you. It is the way you function. And while you are having your thoughts, I am having them too—drawing the information I have about you from my memory banks."

Tracy was reluctant to believe.

"At this instant, you are doubting me," Computer said. "All right—I will prove it. I invite you to attempt to escape. I am a big man, Mr. Tracy—as you were thinking a few moments ago. I am heavy on my feet—another thought of yours. So, you should have no trouble subduing me." He spread his arms. "I invite you to try. Overcome me, Mr. Tracy!"

Tracy leaped across the room.

But Computer had shifted his body slightly, just enough so that Tracy missed him completely. Tracy crashed into the wall, and then slipped to the floor, momentarily stunned.

"How clumsy of you, Mr. Tracy," Computer taunted.

Tracy studied the man. He tried to plan an attack, intending at the last instant to abandon it and try another, but his mind simply would not work that way.

"Yes, that is right—you are a victim of your way of thinking," Computer said. "Your mind works logically, and there is nothing you can do about it. Normally, that is your strength, Mr. Tracy. But in this case it is your weakness."

From a crouching position, Tracy threw himself at Computer again. But, as before, Computer had moved the necessary inches to evade the attack. Tracy slammed against the wall once more.

"Ah, well . . . there is no challenge to the game," Computer said. "It bores me." He moved toward the door, his back to Tracy.

Tracy jumped up and darted after him. He leaped—and clutched empty air and then landed with a thud on the floor.

"Really, Mr. Tracy! Aren't you convinced yet?"

Computer opened the door, smiling the mechanical smile, then stepped out and closed it behind him, locking it again.

Tracy sat up and leaned back against the wall. There seemed to be no defense against Computer's fantastic mind.

He thought about Gustave Moehler—now dead. And that was exactly what Computer had in mind for him too—death. But how? Would Computer commit the murder himself? Or would he assign it to Dutch Borgman? He would probably turn the job over to Borgman. It was too unimportant a matter for Computer to bother himself with. It was a task for a professional killer, not a professional calculator.

Borgman was not a freak, however. He did not have

Computer's mental powers. So there still might be some hope for escape.

His thoughts drifted back to Moehler. And in particular the next door room that Moehler had occupied. Perhaps after the scientist had been taken away the door of the room had been left unlocked. With no prisoner inside, there would be no reason to seal it.

Tracy got to his feet and moved to the wall that separated the two rooms. He leaned his weight against it and it appeared to give. He guessed that it was constructed of wallboard rather than plaster. If that were true, there was a possibility that he could break through it. But . . . if he tried to batter a hole in the wall, Computer and his men might hear.

If he only had some tool . . .

But there was nothing available. His pockets had been emptied.

He would have to try to break through the wall, he decided, and take a chance on Computer or his men hearing. He didn't really have much to lose, since Computer intended to kill him anyway.

Tracy sat on the floor, braced himself, then cocked a leg. He kicked a small hole in the wallboard. He could see the edge of a stud, and the back of the wall in the next door room. Satisfied with his progress so far, he got to his feet and studied the situation. Then he lowered himself to his knees and grasped the ragged edge of the hole. He pulled. There was a ripping sound. He stopped—listening. But he heard nothing. Again, he pulled. A slab of wallboard came loose in his hands.

He sat down again. This time, he put his foot through the hole, placing it against the back of the wall in the next room. He shoved. Again there was a ripping sound. And once more he stopped and listened. But neither Computer nor his men had apparently heard the noise. There was only silence.

Carefully and as quietly as possible, Tracy widened the hole. Before long it was large enough for him to get his shoulders through. Cautiously, he wriggled his way into the next room.

Getting to his feet, he looked around. The room was vacant. The door was closed—but not necessarily locked. There was no sign that Gustave Moehler had ever been there. Tracy would not have known if he had not spoken to him through the wall.

He moved quietly to the door, got hold of the knob, and slowly turned it. The door was not locked! Warily, hoping it would not squeak, he pulled it open. Then he paused and listened. He could see out into the hallway, but, as yet, he could not see to either the right or left. It was possible that either Borgman or Computer's other henchman was waiting for him to appear.

Releasing his hold on the door knob, Tracy leaned forward and peeked out into the hall. He looked to the right—toward where Gustave Moehler had said there was a kitchen. He spotted the kitchen—it was several yards down the hallway—but through the open doorway he saw that there was no one in it standing guard. He glanced to the left. That way was a dead-end.

Tracy stepped out into the hallway. He carefully closed the door behind him, wanting to leave it as he had found it so that it would not cause suspicion. A few yards along the hall, there was a stairway. Tracy could reach it in a half-dozen steps. And, using it, there was a good probability that he could escape.

Yet, he hesitated. If he escaped from Computer, Computer might escape from him. Suppose Tracy managed to get out of the house? And suppose that, minutes later, Computer discovered that he had gone? Computer, then, could flee too, getting away before Tracy could summon help. And if Computer disappeared now, there was little chance that Tracy would find him again before it became too late.

On the other hand, though, Tracy had no weapon. And against him he had the two henchmen, Borgman and the other man, both of whom were armed, as well as Computer, who could anticipate Tracy's every move. His chances of overcoming Computer were practically non-existent. Borgman and the other man were undoubtedly somewhere around. They would spot him and kill him before he ever got a chance to get at Computer.

Still—he had to take the chance. Of what value would his life be—or anyone's life—if Computer succeeded in his plan? Tracy had no real choice. He had to risk himself in order to save his life—and the lives of others.

Tracy moved quietly along the hallway toward the stairs. When he reached the stairway he hesitated again. The temptation to flee was great. But he couldn't run away, he decided; once more, he proceeded, and a few moments later he reached the doorway to the kitchen. He paused to listen intently. There were no sounds in the house. Was it possible that Computer and the other two men had left? No, hardly. Not without killing him first.

He entered the kitchen, and very carefully, he began opening the cupboard drawers hoping that he might find a weapon of some kind. One by one, he found them all completely empty. Puzzling. There was nothing on the counters, and nothing, so far, in the drawers. The kitchen apparently wasn't used. But

Gustave Moehler had mentioned being fed. Where had the food been prepared? Had it been brought in from outside? Or was there another kitchen somewhere in the house? Or did Computer have another hide-out?

He pulled open the last drawer—and stared, surprised. He had found a gun, an automatic. Why would anyone leave his gun in a kitchen drawer? But perhaps it was an extra firearm. That would make sense.

Quietly, he lifted the gun from the drawer. He turned it over in his hands, inspecting it suspiciously. Then he checked it to see if it was loaded—and it was! He was in luck. Now he had the means to combat Computer's brain.

Tracy left the kitchen. Moving on down the corridor he came to a corner. Carefully, he turned it—and found himself facing another stairway, this one going up. That might explain why he had not yet run into Computer's men. They were probably on the second floor. Computer himself would very likely be there too.

He tested his weight on the first step—it creaked. He flattened himself against the wall, waiting and listening, the gun ready. But no one appeared. He moved up to the second step. There was no sound. Then, slowly—very, very slowly—he proceeded up the rest of the steps.

When he reached the next landing he halted again. The hallway ran both to the right and to the left. Which way should he go? There were doors, leading into rooms, presumably, both ways. If he made the wrong choice, if he went the wrong way, he might be stalked from behind. But there was no time to waste hesitating. So he made a quick decision—he turned to the right.

Tracy reached the first door. He listened, but heard nothing inside. In fact, he heard nothing, period, from anywhere on the floor. Could they all be sleeping?

He shoved the door open and stepped into the room, holding the gun ready to fire. The room was furnished—very sparsely—but it was not occupied.

He spent no more time there. He stepped out, closed the door, and crept down the corridor. At the next door, when he listened, he thought he heard breathing—shallow, conscious breathing, as if someone were deliberately trying to keep completely quiet. Or maybe his first guess had been right and for some odd reason they were all asleep.

There was only one sure way of finding out. Gripping the gun tightly, he flung open the door. Then froze, startled.

Computer was seated in the room, facing the doorway, smiling the mechanical smile. Dutch Borgman was standing on his right. And the other man, the smaller one, was standing at his left. They did not appear to be surprised to see Tracy.

"Excellent!" Computer crowed.

Tracy could find no words.

"Perfect!" Computer said. "This has been a test of my powers, Mr. Tracy. And, thanks to your cooperation, it has come off beautifully. Absolutely perfect!" He turned to Borgman. "Eh?" he smiled.

Borgman shook his head in amazement. "You did it," he said. "I didn't see how it could—but you did it. Just like you said, he come right up here, straight as a line."

Tracy was still staring, listening, baffled.

"Surely, you understand," Computer said to him. "I told you—I know exactly how you think. I know exactly what you will do. Let me reconstruct for you your travels from downstairs to this room. I think you'll find it amusing." He shifted slightly in his seat, getting comfortable. "First, of course, you broke through the wall, knowing its thickness, since you had conversed through it with Gustave Moehler. Then, naturally, you made your way to the corridor. Ah, and then . . . then the adventure became interesting. You reached the stairway, and you were tempted to flee. Am I right, so far?"

Tracy nodded.

"You were faced with a choice—or so you imagined," Computer continued. "But, of course, that wasn't the fact. You had no choice at all, Mr. Tracy. It was impossible for you to run away. Because, the way your mind works, you think not only of yourself, but also of others. As a matter of fact, you see it as your duty to protect others before you protect yourself. So . . . do you understand? You had no choice to make. You were forced to proceed—to attempt to stop me, rather than to try to save yourself. I counted on that. I knew it would happen."

Tracy listened, fascinated.

"On to the kitchen, then," Computer continued. "You were puzzled when you found it empty. And it seemed to be unused. But you are thorough, Mr. Tracy. You went through all the drawers, nevertheless. And you were rewarded—you found the gun that I had left for you. A bit of a surprise, wasn't it? But a pleasant surprise. You were exhilarated. You had a means of ending my little plot—or so you imagined. Am I becoming tiresome, Mr. Tracy?"

Tracy shook his head.

"You were suspicious?"

"Yes . . . of course."

"But you found that the gun is loaded. Oh, yes, it's

loaded, all right. Would you like to examine it again to be absolutely certain before you attempt to use it?"

Tracy glanced down at the gun. He tightened his grip on it, and shook his head again.

"Good—then you trust me," Computer grinned. "Well, now, let's see, what next. Oh, yes . . . you made your way up the stairs, then began probing into the rooms—being your typically thorough self—one by one. And, fortunately, you did not have far to search." A dry, humorless grin spread across his face. "And that, Mr. Tracy, is where you came in."

"And what now?" Tracy asked. "I still have the gun."

"So you do. But the game is over. I have no more doubts whatsoever about my abilities. I have proved my power. You, Mr. Tracy, are of no more use to me." He raised a hand and waggled his fingers at Borgman. "Remove him," he ordered.

Borgman stepped forward. At the same time, the other man moved too, heading for Tracy.

Tracy swept the room with the gun. "Hold it!"

Computer laughed—a clattering, metallic-sounding laugh.

Borgman reached into his rear pocket and brought out a pistol.

At the same instant, Tracy fired. The gun barked angrily—once, twice, a third time. But there was no effect. Borgman, with his gun drawn now, closed in. And the smaller man circled toward Tracy's rear.

"Blanks!" Computer clattered. "Blanks, Mr. Tracy!"

Tracy leaped at Borgman, caught him by the wrist, and forced the gun from his hand. It dropped and rattled across the floor. Tracy cocked a right, aiming it, in his mind, for Borgman's jaw. But he was unable to deliver the blow. He felt a sharp crack against his skull—and he dropped, unconscious.

Dimly, Tracy heard the sound of voices. They seemed to be far away, but drawing nearer. He did not move. He felt a pain at the back of his head. But he did not dare reach up to touch the spot. He waited, wondering, waiting, and listening. Then the voice came in clear.

"Don't debate with me," Computer said sharply. "I have no interest whatsoever in the methods you are accustomed to using. You will do this my way. Understand?"

"A dead man is dead," Tracy heard Dutch Borgman reply. "Why go to a lot of trouble for it? Dead is dead."

"I want it to look like an accident," Computer replied. "That is very important. I need more time. I don't want the police looking for Tracy's murderer—and possibly tracing his body to me."

"Okay, okay."

"Be sure you do it exactly as I outlined it. Are you positive that you have every detail clear in your mind?"

"I'm sure, I'm sure."

"Then let's get on with it," Computer snapped.

Tracy felt a foot against his shoulder. Then he was rolled over. Borgman was peering down at him.

"Up!" Borgman commanded. "You're going on your last ride, cop!"

Six

BORGMAN and the other man shoved Tracy from the room, then hurried him down the stairs. When they reached the second flight of steps, they continued downward. A few moments later, they reached a garage below the house. The car was parked there.

The small man got a role of adhesive tape and a pair of handcuffs from the car. Tracy's hands were locked in front of him, then tape was put over his eyes and mouth. He heard the trunk of the car being opened. Then he was shoved roughly into it. A moment later the trunk was slammed closed.

He could hear Borgman and the other man talking.

"The trouble with brains is, it's a lot of trouble for somebody else," Borgman complained. "All Computer does is sit and think. We're the ones that've got to drag this cop all the way up into the mountains to dump him."

"I liked your idea—put a slug in him and kick him out in some alley," the other man said. "No trouble."

Tracy heard the garage door being opened. Then one and then the other car door slammed. After a second, the engine started. The car backed up, then roared forward. They were on their way.

Tracy listened intently again, trying to get some clue to where the hide-out was located. But this time he heard only the sound of other cars, and nothing out of the ordinary.

He began trying to squeeze his hands out of the handcuffs. As he struggled, he began to sweat heavily from the effort. He was breathing fast. After a few minutes he was using up the air in the trunk faster than fresh air was seeping in. He had to stop trying to slip out of the manacles, for fear of using up too much air and suffocating.

After a while the sounds of other cars ceased. They had evidently driven out of the heavy traffic area. The engine of the car sounded as if it was working harder. Tracy guessed that they were going uphill, driving up into the mountains.

In time, the car stopped. He heard Borgman and the other man get out, and then the door of the trunk opened. Tracy was dragged out, and the tape was yanked from his eyes and mouth.

They were back at Gustave Moehler's laboratory. Tracy's car was there, just where he had left it.

"This the end of the line, cop," Borgman said.

"Do you have any objections to telling me how you intend to do this?" Tracy said. "I'm naturally a little interested."

"The hard way," the smaller man replied. "If you got to know, that's how—the hard way."

Borgman pointed past the laboratory building. "Over that way, there's a drop-off," he said. "We're gonna put you behind the wheel of your car, then we're gonna shove the car over the cliff. Computer figures it'll look like you drove off—like an accident, see?"

Tracy raised his hands, smiling. "Handcuffed? Who's going to believe that I drove up into the mountains with my hands in cuffs?"

"There's a road below that cliff," Borgman replied. "That's where the car will land. After it crashes, we'll drive down there and take the cuffs off you. Who's to know you ever had 'em on?"

"We gonna stand around talkin' about it all day?" the other man said gruffly.

Borgman gave Tracy a shove again, aiming him toward his car. "Hop it, cop!"

When they reached the car, the smaller man took Tracy's handcuffs off, then pulled Tracy's arms behind him, and manacled his wrists that way.

Borgman opened the car door. He and the other man inspected the front seat area, making sure there was no hidden weapon. Then the smaller man bound Tracy's legs at the ankles with tape. Next, Tracy was lifted into the front seat of the car and settled behind the steering wheel.

"He could get his feet on the brake," Borgman said. "Computer and his brain—did he figure on that? Maybe he ain't so smart, eh?"

"Here's this gadget here that moves the seat back and forth," the other man said. "I'll tape his feet to it, okay?"

"There you are—now, that's brains," Borgman said approvingly.

The other man bound Tracy's legs tight to the metal handle.

"Nobody could get out of that without a squad of Marines to help him," Borgman said. He reached in and turned the ignition key and switched on the engine. "You got any last words, Tracy?"

Tracy simply made a face of disgust.

"He ain't got nothin' to say—not even a good-bye. Ain't that the way—once a cop, always a cop. Okay, I got something to say to you, then, Tracy—happy landin'!"

Borgman put the gear in 'Drive'. The car inched forward, and he jumped free and then slammed the door closed.

As the car moved slowly away from the two men, headed for the cliff, Tracy tugged frantically to get his legs free. But the tape held. He struggled furiously with the handcuffs. In the rear-view mirror he could see Borgman and the other man watching interestedly. Again, he wrenched his legs, trying to break the bonds. The tape seemed to give a little.

The car was only yards now from the brink of the cliff. Another few seconds and it would go hurtling out into space. Borgman and the other man were following it, moving leisurely, curious—Tracy supposed—to see the smash-up from the top of the cliff. Very near panic, he threw his body sideways, at the same time, twisting his legs violently. The tape snapped! His legs were free!

Tracy struggled back into a sitting position. The car seemed to be poised on the edge of the cliff. Quickly, he raised his knees, found the gear shift, then, as gently as possible, slipped it into the 'Reverse' position.

The car bucked to a sudden halt. The engine hesitated—then caught again. And slowly, slowly the car began inching backwards. In the rearview mirror, Tracy saw that Borgman and the other man were running toward the car. They had their guns drawn. He found the accelerator with his foot and flattened it against the floorboard. The engine roared—and the car rocketed backwards.

Borgman and the other man leaped out of the way.

Tracy slammed on the brake. The car skidded, then came to rest. Tracy lifted his legs and, with his knees, began turning the steering wheel.

There was a shot—a bullet hit the hood of the car and ricocheted, whining.

Tracy hit the accelerator again and the car shot

forward in a half-circle turn. Once more, he stamped on the brake pedal, so that the car skidded dizzily to a stop. Again using his knees, he worked at turning the wheel, trying to turn the car toward the road.

Guns barked. Bullets bit into the car's metal body and glanced, squealing, off the bullet-proof glass.

Tracy stepped hard on the accelerator. This time the car plunged straight for the road.

With a sudden surge of strength, Tracy yanked one hand painfully free of the cuffs. It was numb, but he was able to grab the wheel. He got the accelerator down to the floor, and the car leaped forward.

Borgman's car was in the way, an obstacle between Tracy and the road. He swung his own car sharply to the right, avoiding Borgman's car by bare inches. But he was not able to turn left again quickly enough. His car went roaring upward along the road!

It was a mistake. He was now headed higher up into the mountains, when he should have been driving toward town. But there had been no way of avoiding it. And now he was in trouble because he was unable to turn around on the narrow mountain road.

Tracy zoomed along the road, climbing, climbing. He was not greatly surprised, a few minutes later, to discover that the other car was tailing him. The chase would have to end soon. They would reach the end of the road or the peak of the mountain. And then Tracy would be in almost as much trouble as he had been before. Borgman and the other man had guns. But Tracy was weaponless.

A steep, sheer, rock rise suddenly appeared in front of him. He had reached the end of the road. He slammed the brake and the car wig-wagged, raising a cloud of dust. Fortunately there was space enough to turn around. He put the car in reverse, backed up, then turned in a circle, and sped back down the road.

Suddenly Borgman's car was in front of him. The road was too narrow to accommodate both cars. Tracy would not be able to pass. If he swerved right he would crash into the wall of the mountain. If he swerved left he would go plunging off the road, over the cliff.

But Borgman was faced with the same dilemma. And Tracy elected to force Borgman to make the decision. He aimed his car directly at Borgman's, gripped the wheel firmly, and raced onward.

As the cars neared, Tracy saw the door on the driver's side of the other car suddenly swing open. Then he saw Borgman leap out and go rolling across the road. The car itself, out of control, swung toward the edge of the road, then plunged over the cliff. The other man was trying to escape—but he didn't get out in time. Tracy saw him hurtle downward still in the car.

In his rear-view mirror Tracy watched as Borgman scrambled to his feet, apparently unhurt, and he saw Borgman running toward him. He was raising his gun.

Tracy heard a shot.

The bullet missed the car completely. But Tracy drove on, anyway. Borgman, with a gun, was a danger. And he was not particularly important to Tracy, who was much more interested in getting back to the city to find Computer and stop him.

Tracy radioed headquarters as he headed down the mountain, and talked to the Chief and told him everything that had happened since he had left to go to Gustave Moehler's laboratory. Then he asked the Chief to contact the circus people and find out exactly where their sound truck had been at the time he had heard it, while he was imprisoned in the trunk of Borgman's car.

It was early evening when Tracy finally reached headquarters. He went directly to the Chief's office. Sam was there, too. Tracy dropped into a chair, then raised his arm, dangling the handcuffs.

"Can somebody get me out of this?" he said.

The Chief called down to the garage and asked someone to bring a hammer and chisel. Then he turned back to Tracy.

"I've got the area where that sound truck was operating," he said. "Will it help you?"

"It's the only lead I have," Tracy replied. "I've got to find the house that Computer is using as a hideout. If we work fast enough, we may catch him there. I left Borgman up in the mountains. It will take him a long time to get back. And until he *does* get back, Computer won't know that I got away. He'll think he's safe."

"But it's a big area, it's crowded with houses," Sam said. "How can we find the house that Computer is using?"

"Get me the name and phone number of every real estate dealer in that neighborhood," Tracy said. "Computer is probably renting or leasing the house. One of the real estate men in the area may have handled the deal. If so—he'll remember Computer."

"It's a wild shot," Sam said.

"Just get on it!" Tracy said. "We don't have any spare seconds to play with."

Sam left, and a few minutes later a mechanic from the garage arrived with a mallet and chisel and began hacking away at the handcuffs that were still attached to Tracy's one wrist.

"Give me a little more detail on this Computer,"

the Chief said. "The whole business seems far-fetched to me."

"It wouldn't if you'd been there," Tracy replied. "His mind is fantastic. He can do everything an actual computer can do—and more. He can think."

Finally the handcuffs were removed. Free of that annoyance, Tracy left the Chief's office and went to Sam's desk. Sam was just hanging up the phone.

"Got it," he said. "The Real Estate Dealers Association is sending me a list of its members, with checks beside the names of the dealers in the area we're interested in. It's coming over by messenger—ought to be here in a few minutes."

"We'll have to call every one of them," Tracy said. He looked at his watch. It was still running, even though he had smashed the crystal. "It's getting late," he said. "I hope they'll all be in their offices. If not, we'll have to get their home phones."

"What are we going to ask them?" Sam inquired.

"If they rented or leased a house recently to anyone who fits Computer's description." He suddenly scowled. "But Computer probably didn't arrange for the house himself. He might have sent Borgman to do it. Or—" He shook his head. "No, Computer is too smart for that. He wouldn't have sent Borgman, either. With that eye patch, Borgman would be easily remembered. Maybe he sent the other fellow."

"The one who took a dive off the cliff?" Sam said.

Tracy nodded. "Nobody would ever remember him."

"We're stopped before we even get started," Sam groaned.

"Well, we'll try it, anyway," Tracy said. "We'll ask them all if they recall renting or leasing to either Computer or Borgman. If they say no, then we'll get a list of the houses they've handled over the past few weeks."

"*All* of them?"

"Can you think of any other way to do it?"

Sam sighed and shook his head.

"The house has an inside garage—below the first floor," Tracy said. "That's one way of identifying it. With that to go on, we may not have too much trouble getting a dealer to pinpoint it."

The list of real estate dealers arrived shortly after that, and Sam and Tracy began phoning them immediately.

"This won't be any help," Sam said, hanging up the phone. "That guy told me that that whole area is loaded with one type of house. It's a kind of an English Tudor, built about twenty years ago. And they've all got one thing in common—a lower level garage. There are hundreds and hundreds of them, he says."

"Just keep at it," Tracy ordered.

The telephoning continued until past midnight. At the end of that time, Sam and Tracy had a list of over eighty houses in the area that had been rented during the preceding two weeks.

"Now what—door to door?" Sam asked.

"Right. But let's get some help," Tracy replied. "Round up every officer who can be spared. Give each one of them a few of those addresses. Tell them what we're looking for." He picked up one of the lists. "I'll take this and get started," he said.

"Watch yourself," Sam warned. "Don't forget—Computer knows exactly how you think. He might be waiting for you."

Tracy left headquarters and drove to the first address on his list. The house was dark. But that did not surprise him, since it was nearly one in the morning. He got out of the car and knocked on the door. A few seconds later, a light went on inside the house.

Tracy got out his gun and moved back into the shadows.

The door opened. A middle-aged man—a stranger to Tracy—opened the door and peered out. He was wearing pajamas and a robe.

Tracy put his gun away, then moved out into the light that was coming through the doorway. He identified himself, explained that he had made a mistake, and apologized. The man grumbled a reply, then retreated back into the house.

Approximately the same thing happened at the next two houses. But at the fourth, when Tracy knocked, there was no response at all. He knocked louder. Still, there was no reaction.

He walked around to the rear of the house. He could see that it had a lower level garage. But the door was locked, so he could not determine whether or not there was a car in the garage.

Tracy returned to the front of the house and knocked again—loudly. But still there was no answer. He moved back to the front sidewalk and looked up at the upper stories. There were no lights.

The people might simply be away, he reasoned. He probably should go on to the next address and return here later. But . . . He had a hunch about this house.

He glanced toward the house next door. There was a dim light in on of the upstairs windows—someone still awake, apparently. So he went to the door and knocked. And here he got a response. A few seconds later, a young man appeared.

"Yes?" he said, looking at Tracy puzzledly.

Tracy identified himself. "Actually," he said, "I'm looking for your neighbor. Are they away?"

The young man stuck his head out the door and peered over toward the house next door. "I wouldn't know," he said. "I haven't seen much of them—not anything, come to think of it. They just moved in a few days ago—let's see . . . last week at the end of the week."

"You haven't seen them at all?" Tracy said.

"I'm a student," the young man replied. "I'm in school all day. I was studying, that's why I'm up." He grinned. "Math. I have a lot of trouble with math."

"Your parents, then," Tracy said. "Maybe they've seen them."

"There's only my mother."

"Could you ask her? I'd like to find out where they are. Or, if she doesn't know, ask her if she can describe any of them."

The young man nodded, then went back into the house. He returned a few seconds later. His mother—a plump woman with curlers in her hair—was with him.

"I just wouldn't have no notion," she told Tracy. "A day after they moved in, I went over there. I went up to the door, trying to be neighborly. But I couldn't get a hoot nor a holler out of them. Knocked. Didn't come to the door."

"But you're sure that they've moved in?"

"Oh, sure. I looked out the back window one day and saw one of them taking the car out."

"Could you describe him or her?"

"Him. Nope. Didn't get that good a look. All I saw was that black eye patch."

Tracy grinned. "Thank you . . . thank you very much!"

He returned to the other house and tried the door knob. The door was locked, as he had supposed it would be. He made his way back to his car and contacted Sam by radio.

"I think I've found the place," he said. "Not positive, but pretty close to it."

"I'm having no luck at all," Sam reported. "Unless you can count waking people up out of a sound sleep as luck."

"Let the others continue the search," Tracy ordered. "But you, I want you to get me a search warrant, and bring it here. I don't want to leave here myself. Computer could still be in there."

About forty-five minutes later, Sam arrived with the warrant.

"I'm going around to the rear and try to get in through the garage," Tracy said. "You stay here. I don't want to lose Computer out the front while I'm trying to take him from the back."

"Any sign that he's in there?"

Tracy shook his head. "But that doesn't mean that he isn't," he said. "And if he is, he's expecting me. I've given him plenty of notice that I'm here, the way I've been banging on the door."

"Easy then, Tracy . . ."

Tracy walked to the rear of the house again. When he reached the garage doors, he threw his weight against them. He heard a snapping sound. He had broken the lock. He took out his gun, and held it ready as he opened one of the garage doors. He moved as quietly as he could.

Inside the dark garage he crossed to the back and, feeling his way along, found a doorway. It led to a stairway. Still in darkness, he silently crept upward. When he reached the landing, he paused and listened. There was no sound except the sound of his own breathing.

Tracy used his flashlight for a quick look around. He found a light switch and flicked it on. He was in a corridor—and it looked familiar. Moving toward the front of the house, he located the room in which he had been held. It was easy to identify it by the hole that he had kicked in the wall.

Standing in the hallway, he shouted. "Computer!"

His voice echoed. But there was no answer.

He moved on to the kitchen and switched on the light. It was empty. Then he made his way up the second flight of steps. He found the room that Computer had occupied. It, too, was vacant.

"Tracy searched the rest of the rooms in the house. It did not take him long. He found nothing—not even any evidence that Computer had ever been there. If he had not found the wall with the hole kicked in it, he seriously would have doubted that this was the house where he had been kept a prisoner.

"He's gone," he announced to Sam when he reached the car again.

"Was he here?"

Tracy nodded. "You can call off the search," he said. "This is the house."

"How do you think he knew?"

"Knew what?"

"To leave."

"Borgman must have had some luck. Maybe he got a lift." Tracy replied. "Evidently he got back here before I did."

"Well, I've got some more bad news for you," Sam said. "It came in on the radio while you were in the house. Gustave Moehler's body was found. He'd been shot and dumped in an alley."

Tracy nodded sadly. "Borgman's work. That's what he wanted to do with me."

"Any idea where they went?" Sam said.

"None. Absolutely none, Sam. They could be anywhere. They might not even still be in this country."

Sam gestured wearily. "Well . . . we tried . . ."

"That wasn't good enough. And we can't stop now. We'll have to think of something else."

"Sure . . ." Sam said defeatedly.

"There's a way . . . a way of finding him again," Tracy was determined.

"Out-think him?" Sam smiled. "How? You said yourself, Tracy, he's a computer."

Tracy shook his head. "He has the capability of a computer. But he *isn't* a computer, Sam. He's a human being. He has a weakness. Or his plan has a weakness. I just have to find it, that's all."

Sam yawned. "Maybe if we sleep on it?" he suggested.

Tracy replied grimly, "I just hope there's time for that."

Seven

WHEN TRACY arrived at headquarters the next morning he looked much the same as he had when Sam and he had parted the night before.

"You were supposed to sleep," Sam said.

"With Computer on my mind?" He shook his head. "But I have an idea. I may be able to draw Computer out of hiding."

He telephoned Dr. Zgani and made an appointment to see him, explaining to the scientist that he needed his cooperation in an attempt to smoke out the man who had had him abducted.

A few minutes later, as Sam and Tracy drove toward Dr. Zgani's office, Sam said, "Do you expect Zgani to remember something? His mind was a total blank as far as that twenty-four hours was concerned."

"No, that's not it," Tracy replied. "I want to use him as bait. I want Computer to try to kidnap him again."

"Why should he?" Sam said. "He already knows everything that Zgani knows."

"Correction," Tracy smiled. "He knows everything that Dr. Zgani knew at the time of the abduction. But what about since then?"

Sam thought a moment, then nodded. "I see what you're getting at," he said. "And . . . it might work."

When they reached Dr. Zgani's laboratory they were escorted into his private office immediately. Then Tracy told Dr. Zgani everything that had occurred since they had last talked.

"It's all very difficult to comprehend," Dr. Zgani frowned. "A man with a computer mind . . . Gustave Moehler's drug . . . it borders very close on the unbelievable."

"It'll be believable, all right, if Computer isn't stopped," Tracy said.

Zgani nodded gloomily. "Yes . . . yes, I can see that. But what can I do? How can I help you?"

"I want you to announce a new and very important advance in some area of your work," Tracy replied.

Zgani looked at him blankly. "There is no such discovery that I know of," he said.

"Nevertheless, I want you to make an announcement to that effect."

Dr. Zgani stiffened. "I am afraid that that is out of the question," he replied. "Science does not announce findings that do not exist."

"I realize that," Tracy replied. "But this is necessary. Somehow, I have to draw Computer out of hiding. If you—"

"Impossible," Dr. Zgani interrupted.

"Then, would you consider this?" Tracy said. "Woud you make an announcement that you intend to make an announcement?"

"Pardon?"

"Send out a notice to the newspapers, saying that you intend to hold a press conference at which you will make an announcement concerning an important break-through in . . . in whatever field you care to choose. Would you do that?"

Dr. Zgani considered for a second. "And when the time for this press conference arrives and I have nothing to announce, then what?"

"You could set it for a week or so ahead. By that time, if my idea works, we'll have Computer under arrest. You can call the press conference off. Or we can explain to the papers why we called it."

Dr. Zgani considered again. Then he said, "How exactly is this going to help you?"

"At this point," Tracy replied, "Computer thinks he knows everything you know. He has your knowledge stored in his memory banks. But suppose you *did* come up with a new finding in some area of science? His knowledge, then, would be incomplete."

"That's correct," Zgani nodded. "Until he knew what I knew."

"I think Computer would make an attempt to get that new knowledge," Tracy said. "He's not as sure of himself as he would like us to believe. At least, that's my guess. I think he would try to abduct you again—to add the new knowledge to what he already has."

"And we would be prepared for that, I imagine," Dr. Zgani said.

"Either Sam or I will be watching you every minute," Tracy replied. "We'll make sure that you're not harmed."

"Computer will probably send his strong-arm man to pick you up," Sam said. "But we can handle him. Instead of him getting you, we'll get him."

"And—hopefully—he will lead you to Computer?"

"That's my idea," Tracy nodded. "Will you help us?"

"It will be very difficult," Dr. Zgani scowled. "To have the newspapers expect an announcement of a finding and then to . . ." He shrugged. "All right, yes, I will do it."

"Let's just hope that Computer reads the papers," Sam said.

The announcement—that Dr. Zgani would soon reveal an important discovery in the field of laser research—appeared in the city's newspapers the following day. Tracy immediately assigned himself to guard Dr. Zgani. He spent the rest of the day in his car, sitting outside Zgani's laboratory, watching, expecting Dutch Borgman to appear. But, no luck.

That evening when Dr. Zgani left the lab, Tracy followed him. He trailed his car up into the hills, and watched as Zgani opened the gate to his property. After Zgani was safe inside, Tracy parked in the trees near the gate and spent the night watching and waiting. Still, however, nothing happened.

Sam took over the watch the next morning. And Tracy, for the first time in many hours, slept. But when he relieved Sam that afternoon, Sam had nothing of interest to report.

"People come and go," Sam said, indicating the laboratory, "but none of them are Borgman—or Computer."

"Well, that's what a stake-out is—dull," Tracy said.

Two more days passed, with Tracy and Sam keeping Dr. Zgani under surveillance every second of the time. And with only one more day left before he was scheduled to make the important announcement, Zgani became nervous. He called Tracy in.

"I want to cancel the press conference," he said. "This isn't working. I have to think about my reputation. What will other scientists say when they learn that I have nothing to announce?"

"Give us one more day," Tracy replied.

Zgani shook his head. "I never should have agreed to this. Computer somehow knows what you are attempting. He is not going to be fooled."

"I'm beginning to suspect that that's right," Tracy replied. "But, we've gone this far—let's follow through. What difference will one more day make to you?"

Zgani groaned. "It's just nonsense."

"One more day," Tracy pleaded.

"All right . . . all right . . . but . . . but it's nonsense."

Tracy returned to his car. It was mid-afternoon, and he would be on duty until the following morning. But, like Dr. Zgani, he now had little expectation that the attempt at kidnapping would be made. It seemed that Computer, knowing how Tracy's mind worked, had understood the trick.

Nevertheless, Tracy followed Dr. Zgani home that evening, and then, after Zgani had passed through the gate, parked his car in the woods and continued the vigil. To his surprise, he soon got action. But it was not what he had expected.

As he was sitting in the car, his door was suddenly yanked open. He turned, startled, and found himself facing the muzzle of a pistol. It was being held by Dutch Borgman.

"Out, cop!" Borgman snapped.

Tracy climbed out of the car.

Borgman pointed down the road. "March!"

As they proceeded, Tracy said, "Let me guess–you intend to kill me, then go back after Dr. Zgani–right?"

"You're only about a thousand miles off," Borgman retorted. "Computer ain't got no interest in Zgani. You're the one he wants."

"But Dr. Zgani's new discovery . . . isn't Computer –"

"You think you fooled him with that?" Borgman snarled. "One thing you forgot. He knows what Zgani knows. And what Zgani knows is that he ain't nowhere near making no new discovery on nothing."

"Yes . . . that was a mistake on my part."

"The last mistake you're ever going to make, too, cop. Computer ain't amused by you no more."

They reached a car that was parked on the road. Borgman took Tracy's gun, then ordered him into the car. He had Tracy drive, while Borgman sat beside him, pointing his gun at him. They headed back toward the city.

"Isn't this a waste of your time?" Tracy said. "Why didn't you kill me back there? That's your way, as I understand it."

"I booted it last time," Borgman replied. "Computer don't figure to let that happen again. He wants to be on the spot when I knock you off. He don't want no more slip-ups."

"You mean he doesn't trust you."

"I don't mean nothing like that."

"But, the fact is, he *doesn't* trust you, does he?"

"He's got me working with him, ain't he?"

"Temporarily, yes—while he can use you. But what will happen when he no longer needs you, Borgman? He won't always need a strong-arm man. And you're a bungler. You said so yourself—you said you booted it. How long will Computer keep you around after he no longer needs you?"

Borgman laughed. "Boy, does Computer know how you think!" he said. "He told me this'd happen. He told me you'd try to swing me around, turn me against him. He's really got you pegged. You can't think a thought but what he don't know it. You know—he knows more about what you know than you know yourself. You just ain't got no chance against him. None."

Tracy fell silent.

They returned to the section of the city where the

warehouses were located. Borgman had Tracy park the car at the rear of one of the buildings, then ordered him out.

"This is the new hide-out, I assume," Tracy said.

"Yeah, this is one place Computer's got. But he's got more. He's ready for anything. It don't take much for us to move, you know. Everything we got that's important is right up there in Computer's head. Where he goes, it goes. You can't beat a setup like that."

"Apparently not," Tracy replied.

Still holding the gun on Tracy, Borgman opened the rear door of the building. "In," he commanded.

Tracy stepped through the doorway. It was dark inside.

"Okay, now hold it," Borgman said. He got a small flashlight from his rear pocket, switched it on, then turned his attention back to the door, intending to lock it.

At that instant—when Borgman's attention was divided—Tracy suddenly kicked out at the flashlight. He caught it with the toe of his shoe and it went flying.

"You—!" Borgman cried, angry.

Tracy dived into the darkness. He crashed into something solid, and fell, a pain shooting up his right leg. In spite of the injury, he scrambled to his feet and charged headlong into the darkness once more. Then, again, he met with an obstacle and crashed to the floor.

Borgman had retrieved the flashlight. The beam swept the interior of the building, searching for Tracy.

"You can't get out of here!" Borgman raged. "You're dead, Tracy!"

Tracy crawled behind the object he had fallen over. From hiding, he followed the beam of the light. He saw the head of a wooden horse, painted garish colors. And then a fire engine—child's size. For a moment he was puzzled, then he realized that the warehouse was used to store carnival equipment.

The light skimmed past Tracy. He was hiding in the seat of a Ferris wheel. It would be little protection if Borgman got any closer.

"You're in a hole, Tracy!" Borgman shouted. "You can't get out!"

The light swept past him again. Borgman was moving in Tracy's direction. Silently, he slipped down out of the seat, and, on hands and knees, slowly retreated.

"I got you cornered, Tracy!" Borgman shouted.

But Tracy knew he was bluffing.

Tracy's head bumped into something hard and solid. He was stunned for an instant. And in that instant, the light found him. He jumped up and lunged into darkness again just as a shot was fired. The bullet hit metal and screamed and then hit glass. The glass shattered.

Tracy fell again—fortunately, for the light kept going and lost him. He crouched, listening. He could hear Borgman's movements. He was closing in on the spot where Tracy had fallen. Once more, the light skipped by Tracy, overhead.

In the light beam, Tracy saw a metal, scaffold-like structure. It looked like part of the track for a roller coaster. If he could climb it he might get out of the path of Borgman's flashlight. Borgman would not expect him to be anywhere off the floor.

He inched his way through the darkness toward the base of the structure. His foot caught on something—

the something toppled, and there was a clattering sound. The light immediately speared through the darkness in Tracy's direction. There was another shot. The bullet ricocheted wildly, creating a racket of banging and clanging. Tracy froze and waited. The beam of light passed near him, hesitated, played in his vicinity, then moved slowly on.

Once more, Tracy crawled forward. His hand fell on something loose, a little larger than his fist. He felt it, determining its shape, and decided it was a cap for the end of an axle. Raising his head, he saw that the light was concentrating on an area a few yards away. But it would be back his way soon, he was sure.

Hoping to get Borgman's attention away from him, Tracy stood up in the darkness and hurled the object he had found toward the far end of the warehouse. It landed, bounced, and then clattered over metal.

Four rapid shots flashed in the darkness—all aimed in the direction Tracy had thrown the object. Then the light beamed, moved quickly toward the far end of the building. The ruse had worked.

Moving fast but quietly, Tracy climbed the rails of the roller coaster. He rose higher and higher. And then suddenly his hand slipped. He lost his grip and fell—and dangled by one hand. Looking toward the spot where the light was shining, he saw it turn back in his direction. Apparently he had made some sound. He dared not move now.

Hanging from the tracks, he watched as the light returned. But it was low, skimming over the tops of the pieces of equipment. It stayed low. Borgman obviously did not know exactly where the new sound had come from.

Tracy's grip was loosening. His hand, perspiring, was slipping from the rail. But if he moved to try to get a grip with the other hand the action might draw Borgman's attention. He had to hold on, at least until the last instant when maintaining the grip would be impossible.

The light moved closer, still swinging back and forth, covering the width of the warehouse, but remaining low. Tracy's hold slipped another notch. He was gripping the track now with only the tips of his fingers. His arm ached. His body felt as if it weighed a ton.

Borgman was almost directly under Tracy now. Almost—but not exactly. He was still a foot or so to the left. If only he would move in the right direction. If only—

At that instant, Tracy lost his hold. He went hurtling downward. And at the same moment, Borgman moved on, stepping out of Tracy's reach. Tracy hit the floor with a thud and fell to his knees. Borgman, hearing the sound, swung around. The light picked Tracy up in its beam. Tracy saw Borgman's gun come up. He dived—low, at Borgman's legs. The gun barked—once, twice, three times. But Tracy was not hit. He had crashed into Borgman, but then had lost his hold on him. Borgman scrambled to his feet noisily, and spun around. He searched for Tracy with the light—and found him. He raised his gun to shoot. Tracy heard a click, click, click. Borgman's gun was empty.

Now, Tracy decided, he had a chance! He lunged toward the light. But it disappeared. Borgman had switched it off. Tracy floundered in the darkness. He heard a clicking sound again. He recognized it and knew what Borgman was doing—he was reloading his gun. The chance had been lost. Tracy dived into the darkness again, fleeing.

Abruptly, the light flashed on again. And at the same instant a bullet sang through the air. Tracy dropped and skidded along the floor. The light followed. He rose, leaped behind a merry-go-round seat, and then heard a shot and felt a bullet smack into it. Once more, he ran. The light picked him up—then lost him—then found him. He ducked down.

The light came looking for him, poking into corners. He waited, trying to control his breathing, fearful of making any sound at all. The beam of the light flashed on a mirror that was standing nearby, looking distorted. Tracy guessed that it was a mirror from a fun house.

Borgman was closing in again. Tracy could hear his footfalls clearly. He hesitated. Was it too late to run again? It was! Borgman was almost upon him. And then suddenly the fun house mirror reflected both the light and Borgman's figure. Borgman looked fat and bloated above the waist and skinny and emaciated below the waist. But, oddly, he did not even glance at the reflection of himself in the mirror. If he had, he would have seen Tracy, crouched down at the base of the mirror.

Borgman moved on.

Tracy was so surprised that he almost spoke to him. And then he realized what had happened. Borgman had had his blind side toward the mirror—he actually had not seen his reflection. Tracy grasped the knowledge—and used it. He moved out, following Borgman, stepping quietly, using the fall-out from the beam of light to see by, keeping to Borgman's blind side.

Tracy spotted a doorway. Borgman reached it and passed it. Tracy reached it—and stepped through it. Once more he was in darkness. And Borgman had gone on.

He felt his way along the wall. He seemed to be in a corridor. Where did it lead? Out—out to the street? Then he stumbled. He had reached a stairway. He waited, listening, hoping that Borgman had not heard the sound. He could hear no sign that Borgman was returning.

The stairs were a disappointment. They led upward, not toward the street. But upward—or anywhere—was preferable, he decided, to facing Borgman and the gun. So, quietly, he moved up the steps. And soon he reached a second floor.

Suddenly, below him he saw Borgman's light. Tracy was on some sort of balcony. He could watch the beam of light darting in and out among the pieces of equipment. Borgman now had no idea where Tracy was hiding.

Perhaps there was a way up to the roof from this balcony. It was possible. He had to explore *every* possibility, for death was waiting for him on the floor below.

Cautiously, Tracy made his way along the balcony. The light suddenly beamed upward. He pulled back to avoid being seen. Had Borgman heard him? Or guessed that he had found his way to the stairs? Tracy pressed himself flat against the wall and moved slowly on, hoping to stay clear of the light.

He reached a closed door. He turned the knob and looked in—into more darkness. Closing the door, he proceeded. A moment later he came to another door. Evidently there were rooms all along the balcony. But which one—if any—might lead him to the roof?

Out of the corner of his eye, Tracy saw the light again. It was behind him. Borgman had climbed the stairs to the balcony. Tracy darted forward, found the next door, flung it open—and stepped into a blaze of light. He was in a brightly lighted room, face to face with Computer. The big man sat behind a shiny desk.

"Mr. Tracy!" Computer smiled brittlely. "A bit late—but better late than never, eh?"

Tracy whipped around to flee and found himself confronted by Borgman, who stood blocking the doorway. Borgman's gun was aimed at Tracy.

"Trouble, I assume," Computer said to Borgman. "I heard the gunfire. But, of course, the best place to be when there is gunfire is where the gunfire isn't. So I remained here."

"He . . . uh, got away from me there for a minute," Borgman said sheepishly. "But he's here—okay? So what's the beef?"

"Absolutely correct. He is here. And this time there will be no errors."

Borgman moved from behind Tracy and into the room.

"You have been a great deal of trouble to me, Mr. Tracy," Computer said wearily. "Too, you disturb me. Knowing your mind, I am greatly agitated by it. You are truly a remarkable thinker—that is, in one particular sense. Your ability to analyze—to find the nub of the matter—is quite astonishing. For instance, you *did* find my house—my previous hideout, I imagine."

Tracy nodded.

"Yes . . . I knew you would. When Mr. Borgman returned and told me that you had escaped, I was certain that it would not be long before you put in an appearance. So, naturally, we left."

"I figured that out when I didn't find you there," Tracy replied sourly.

"Yes, of course. Tell me, how exactly did you locate the house?"

"I called the real estate brokers in—"

"Yes, yes, I know that—that's elementary. My question is, how did you know which neighborhood the house was located in?"

"I heard a sound truck while Borgman was carrying me in the trunk of the car," Tracy replied. "When I got free, I checked to find out where the sound truck was when I heard it."

"You knew exactly what time you heard it?"

"I broke the crystal on my watch and felt the hands. It was a guess."

"But an excellent guess. And I am not surprised. As I said, you have a remarkable mind. It is a shame that you cannot join me in my enterprise. I could use you. You would be so superior to—" He glanced toward Borgman. "—so superior to some others."

"No thanks," Tracy said.

"Oh, I had no hope of recruiting you. I know too well how you think. You believe that what I intend to do is a crime—you believe it completely. I suppose I could change your way of thinking. If I were inclined to do so. But it would be a great deal of bother. And I simply don't choose to waste time on the matter. So . . ."

"So, are you gonna talk him to death, or are you gonna let me handle it?" Borgman said gruffly.

"Mr. Borgman is impatient—one of his drawbacks," Computer said to Tracy.

"We brought him here to bump him off, didn't we?" Borgman insisted.

"Quite correct."

"Okay, then."

"Correct, again. We have wasted much too much time on Mr. Tracy. You may proceed, Mr. Borgman."

"Here? Now?" Borgman said, not sure.

"Of course . . . here and now. I want to see it. I want to make sure that it is done."

"Right," Borgman nodded. He raised his gun and aimed it straight at Tracy's head.

"Regrets, Mr. Tracy," Computer said. He turned to Borgman again. "Any time your trigger finger is ready," he said.

Eight

TRACY STARED straight back at the little round hole of the muzzle that was pointed at him. Calmly, addressing Computer, he said, "I mentioned this before—I told you that I suspected you would make a mistake, just as all the would-be world-conquerers before you have made mistakes." He nodded toward the gun. "This is your mistake."

For a moment, Computer showed no reaction. Then he lifted a hand, signalling to Borgman. "Just a moment . . ." he said. He eyed Tracy curiously. "Exactly *what* is my mistake?"

"You'll find out later," Tracy replied.

"You're bluffing!" Computer snapped.

Tracy peered at him blandly. "Why would I do that? What good would it do me? You're going to kill me anyway. I mentioned your mistake because I want you to know—when *you* find out about it—that I realized you were making it before you did."

"Are you gonna listen to that jabber?" Borgman said gruffly to Computer. "Let's get this over with!"

"Lower that gun!" Computer growled at him. He faced back to Tracy. "What mistake?"

"I see no reason why I should satisfy your curiosity," Tracy replied coldly. "I have nothing to gain. If I tell you what you're doing wrong, you'll correct the error. But it won't help me. You'll still kill me. You have to kill me. I'm a danger to you as long as I'm alive."

"Then killing you isn't the mistake?"

Tracy did not reply.

Computer turned to Borgman again. "Find out!" he commanded.

"Find out what?"

"What I'm doing wrong!" Computer raged. Color rushed into his face. He squeezed his hands into fists, trying to control his anger.

"You know what he's thinking," Borgman replied. "Ask yourself."

"It doesn't compute," Computer snarled. "I'm not getting a clear-cut answer. There's something wrong—very wrong. He's—I don't know."

Borgman looked at him worriedly. "What're you talking about? You said you could figure out everything he was thinking. Can you or can't you?"

"Of course I can. I've proved it!"

"So prove it again," Borgman insisted. "Is he bluffing or ain't he?"

"Don't order me to do anything!" Computer snarled. "I'll let you know when I'm putting you in charge. Until then, don't *give* orders—*follow* orders!" He swung back to Tracy. "Out with it! Tell me! What is the mistake?"

Tracy shook his head. "You won't get anything out of me."

"You *are* bluffing!" Computer snapped. "It's computing now. Yes, I see . . . it was a trick."

"A trick to what?" Borgman asked.

"Yes, a trick to what?" Tracy smiled.

Once more, a pinkness flooded Computer's face. He muttered something, a garble of words, then turned his back to Tracy and Borgman.

"I ask you again—do you know what he's thinking or don't you?" Borgman said sharply.

"I want you to find out," Computer replied. "I command you."

"What?"

"Find out! Find out what the mistake is!"

"Then you don't know what he's thinking."

"Find out! Find out!"

Borgman made a face of disgust. Then, holding the gun on Tracy, he moved in on him. "You just hold still, cop, and take it," he said. "You fight back, and you get a bullet."

Tracy raised his hands. "Never mind—that isn't necessary. I'll tell him the mistake he's made. It's too late to correct it now, anyway."

Computer whipped around, facing Tracy again "Talk!"

"It was a simple, obvious error," Tracy said. "You assumed that I was alone when I was shadowing Dr. Zgani. But wouldn't that have been a little foolish of me? I knew you wouldn't fall for my trick—Dr. Zgani's announcement that he had made an important discovery. Because, knowing how my mind works, you would realize that it was a trick. So—playing a hunch—I guessed that you would send Borgman to get me."

"And I got you," Borgman said. "What's a mistake about that?"

"He had himself watched, you fool!" Computer shouted.

"Correct," Tracy smiled. "While I was shadowing Dr. Zgani, one of my men was following me. I have no doubt that he trailed us here to this warehouse. If you'll take a look, I think you'll find him outside. And, I'm sure that by now he has radioed for a squad of men. You should have visitors very soon."

"That's wild!" Borgman said. "Nobody followed us

here. If he called for men, how come it's taking them so long to get here?" He turned to Computer. "You don't believe that guff, do you?"

"It's possible!" Computer snarled.

"Sure, anything's possible. But it don't make no sense. Look in your head—whattaya see? You know how he thinks. He's bluffing, right?"

"Get him out of here!" Computer ordered.

"What?"

"I said, get him out of here! The police have nothing against us, so far—no proof of anything. But if a raiding party broke in here and found his body—or even him, alive—they could lodge a charge against us —abduction. Take him out of here! Somewhere! I don't care—anywhere."

"And what?" Borgman asked.

"And kill him. But do it in some way so that there will be no trace of him. I need more time. I can't be bothered by an investigation. Make sure that his body isn't found."

"You know, this is crazy," Borgman said disgustedly. "He didn't have nobody following us."

"Maybe not. But I can't take the chance. Too much is at stake. Do as I told you—get him out of here!"

"What about you?"

"I'm getting out, too," Computer replied. He moved toward the door. "I'll be at the other place. When you finish with him, meet me there."

"Listen—" Borgman protested.

But Computer was gone, hurrying out the door, moving as rapidly as his heavy weight would allow him to move.

Borgman shook his head, irked. "Of all the nutty . . ."

"He doesn't seem as sure of himself as he once did,

does he?" Tracy smiled. "Did he strike you—chasing out of here—as the kind of man who might conquer the world?"

"Just keep shut!" Borgman growled. He gestured with the gun. "Let's get out of here. You first. And I've got this rod on you, don't forget it!"

Tracy left the room, with Borgman following him. Borgman switched on the flashlight and lighted their way down the stairs and then across the warehouse and out the door. When they reached the street, he commanded Tracy to halt.

"Where's the cop that followed us?" he said, looking up and down the street.

Tracy looked too. "He doesn't seem to be around. Do you suppose I was wrong?"

"Nutty! The whole works is nutty!" Borgman grumbled.

"Why don't we go to the place where you're supposed to meet Computer and tell him that," Tracy suggested.

"Knock it off!" He prodded Tracy with the gun. "Over to the car!"

They crossed to Borgman's car. As before, Tracy got in behind the wheel, and Borgman sat beside him, holding the gun on him.

"Pull out," Borgman ordered.

They drove for several blocks, turning one corner after another. Borgman kept a watch out the rear window, checking to be sure that they were not being followed. Finally, he ordered Tracy to pull over to the curb.

"I got to dope out how to get rid of you," he said when the car stopped. "It's got to be some way so nobody'll find your body."

"Don't expect me to help," Tracy replied.

Borgman pondered, making troubled faces. It was clear that he wasn't used to doing much thinking.

"Computer makes things too complicated," Tracy said. "What difference does it make whether my body is found or not?"

"Don't bug me!" Borgman snarled. Then he suddenly broke into a grin. "Yeah . . . that's it," he said. "I got it. That way, there ain't nobody gonna find your body never. Okay—drive straight. I'll tell you when to turn."

Tracy did as he was told.

"You ever been in a steel mill?" Borgman said, grinning, clearly enjoying his thoughts.

"Not that I recall."

"I used to work in a steel mill. That's where I lost my eye. You're gonna see one tonight—a mill. That's where we're going."

"A big mill? With plenty of places to hide a body."

Borgman laughed. "Yeah . . . one place I got in mind . . ." He touched the patch over his eye. "I got a splash of hot steel right here," he said. "Burned my eye out. There wasn't nothing left of it." He pointed. "Take a right at the next corner."

"Is that what I have in store for me?"

"You got it figured right. I'm gonna show you how it is in a steel mill. What they do is, see, they mix up this hot steel in these vats—big tubs of hot, liquid steel."

"Interesting."

"These vats, they got a kind of bridge across them. You can get up on that bridge, and you can look down and see all that hot, soupy steel. Anything dropped into it, it just disappears. Get the idea? It's just gone. Nobody ever knows what happened to it."

"Fascinating."

"Yeah. You drop something in that steel, see, and it melts kind of and becomes part of the steel. It's there. You can't see it, but it's there—part of the steel. I mean, get the picture? Like say you. Say you was dropped into a vat of that steel. Later on, you'd be poured out and cooled off and made into steel bars or wire or something. Then you'd be sold to somebody that uses steel to make things. Maybe an automobile company. Say you was dropped into a vat. You could end up, six months or a year from now, driving down this same street. Only not at the wheel like you are now. As part of the car—get it?"

"I get it," Tracy replied.

"You don't get the joke of it, though, eh?"

"Very funny," Tracy answered grimly.

"I got to remember that to tell Computer. He'll get a kick out of that."

"Apparently you think the steel company is going to let you walk in and drop me into a vat," Tracy said. "Don't they have a rule against that?"

"I told you—I used to work there. I know my way around. Anybody that used to work there can get in and out of the place without being seen. The guys who work there want to take off for a couple hours or so, maybe for some reason, they can slip out. Some other guy covers for them."

"Aren't there people working there?" Tracy said. "Won't *some*body see us?"

"Only guys I got to worry about is the guys tending the furnaces. See, you can't let steel cool off. Anyway, not until you're ready for it to cool off. So they keep the furnaces going all the time. That was the job I had. I worked on a furnace."

"The furnace tenders will spot us," Tracy said.

"I don't figure it. Nope. I recall how it was. You're

down there at the furnace, and you got these big thick goggles over your eyes to protect you from the heat. You don't never look up. And that bridge I was telling you about is up—away up high over the vats. So, when you're tending the furnaces you don't see nothing but that big blast of flame that's right in front of your eyes." He indicated the patch again. "That's how it happened to me. I took off my goggles once. It was a big mistake."

Tracy was silent for a moment. "I don't think I want to be boiled alive in a vat of molten steel," he said.

"You ain't got no say about it. Alive or dead, that's what's coming up for you. You try to jump me, and I'll plug you right here. It don't make much difference to me whether you climb up to that bridge under your own power or I drag you up—dead. Getting rid of your body, that's all that matters to me."

Now it was Tracy who did some pondering. He decided that at the moment he had little chance of escaping alive. If he made any unusual move at all, Borgman would surely fire the gun. And he could not miss at this near distance. All Tracy could do was wait it out, and hope for some opportunity later.

"Up ahead—see?" Borgman said. "Where the sky is kind of an orange color. That's the steel mill. That's the gases from the furnaces burning, that color. We'll be there in a couple minutes."

Tracy considered stepping down hard on the accelerator and driving the car into a lamp post. But he knew that Borgman would shoot. And even if Borgman missed they might both be killed in the crash.

Perhaps Borgman's luck was due to run out. Maybe someone would notice Borgman taking him into the mill, holding a gun on him. The possibility, he decided, was worth waiting for. It carried less risk than crashing the car.

"Turn left up here," Borgman said.

Tracy made the turn. He could see the outline of the factory buildings against the early morning sky. A tall chimney was belching the burning gases into the atmosphere.

"About the middle of the block," Borgman said, "Pull up and stop."

When they reached the place Borgman had indicated, Tracy guided the car to the curb and parked. Borgman reached across, turned off the ignition, removed the key and put it into his pocket.

"It don't pay to take chances," he said. "In this neighborhood, a guy could get his car stole." He got out of the car, then motioned for Tracy to get out too.

They were standing beside a chain-link fence.

"Move," Borgman said, pointing. "There's a hole in the fence somewhere along here."

A moment later, Borgman called Tracy to a halt. He reached down, keeping an eye on Tracy, and tugged at the fence. The wire separated from the post, leaving an opening.

"Okay–in through here."

Tracy bent down, then crawled through the hole. Borgman followed. Tracy looked up at the windows of the mill, and realized they were dark. The place seemed deserted.

"That way," Borgman pointed.

Tracy, following directions, led the way across an open space toward the buildings.

"The only guard they got is at the main entrance,"

Borgman said. "There ain't many people that's interested in breaking into a steel mill, you know."

"There are offices, aren't there?"

"Oh, yeah, they got guards inside. But the way we're going, we're going around them."

They reached the buildings.

"Over here," Borgman said. "Down these steps."

Tracy saw some cement steps that led downward. He went down them, with Borgman close at his heels. A moment later he came to a door.

"Open it."

The door was unlocked. Tracy pushed it open, then stepped into a dimly-lighted room. It was stacked high with pasteboard cartons. Borgman prodded him in the back with the gun.

Tracy moved forward and came to another door. It, too, was unlocked, and opened onto a long corridor.

"Which way?" Tracy asked.

"Let me get my bearings. It's been a couple years since I been in here."

"No hurry," Tracy said.

"Okay—I got it." He pointed. "That way. And, from now on, no more talk."

Perhaps there was a good possibility of running into a guard, Tracy decided, as they proceeded along the corridor. Otherwise, why would Borgman have commanded silence?

They were coming to a corridor that crossed the one they were in. Borgman nudged Tracy with the gun, then used it to point, indicating that Tracy should turn left into the connecting corridor.

They made the turn. Ahead was an iron stairway.

Tracy looked for something to use as a weapon.

Ahead, attached to the wall, he saw a large fire extinguisher. If he grabbed it, perhaps—

But as they neared the piece of fire equipment, Tracy felt the gun in his ribs. Borgman had guessed what he had considered doing.

They reached the stairway and climbed upward. After a moment they came to another door.

"In!"

Tracy turned the knob, and pushed open the door, and was immediately hit by a wave of heat. He saw that they had entered the main processing area of the mill.

The section was lighted by a fiery glow from the furnaces. Tracy could see the vats, with a vaporous steam rising from them. They were mammoth. The whole place had a nightmare look of the lower regions.

Again, Borgman prodded Tracy with the gun, urging him onward. They crossed the floor toward the furnaces. The sound of the fires was overwhelming. Tracy knew that it would be pointless to shout for help—his voice would never be heard. He looked up—and saw the bridges that Borgman had mentioned. They were built high over the steaming vats.

They came to a ladder that climbed to one of the bridges. Borgman said something to Tracy, but Tracy could not hear what it was. Then Borgman gestured angrily with the gun, indicating that Tracy should climb the ladder.

Tracy hesitated an instant. Was this his last chance to make a move?

He saw Borgman grip the gun nervously.

Tracy elected to wait a while longer. Maybe, climbing the ladder, he could kick back at Borgman and catch him off guard.

He started up, glancing back after almost every step. But, again, Borgman was expecting an attack. He remained several steps behind Tracy, out of range of a kick.

Tracy reached the bridge. Again, he looked back. Borgman had halted. He motioned with the gun, telling Tracy to move on, out further on the span. And he did not complete the climb until Tracy had obeyed and was out of his way.

The heat rising over the vat was almost unbearable. Tracy looked over the railing, down into the bubbling, molten steel. A sickening feeling came over him. He could see the men at the furnaces. But Borgman was right, there was little chance that any of them would look up. They were involved in their work, standing at the furnaces, bare to the waist, goggles clamped to their eyes. Tracy could drop into the vat and there was little chance that they would even know about it. There was absolutely no chance now that any of them could stop Borgman. It was too late.

Borgman was standing behind Tracy. He touched him on the shoulder with the gun. Tracy turned to face him. An evil grin spread across Borgman's face. Tracy knew that the time had come.

He cocked himself, intending to throw himself at Borgman, even though he knew that the effort would be useless. But at that instant something happened. He and Borgman both saw it. One of the men at the furnaces reached up and removed his goggles.

Tracy saw the color drain from Borgman's face. He was evidently remembering his own accident. Without realizing what he was doing, Borgman turned, taking his eyes from Tracy, and shouted down at the man at the furnace, crying a warning.

Tracy leaped forward, landing on Borgman. Borgman became aware of his mistake and fought back. He raised the gun and brought it down, using it as a club. But he missed. His arm hit the railing. The gun dropped from his hand and plunged down into the vat of molten steel.

Raging, Borgman threw Tracy away from him. Tracy landed on his back and skidded backwards along the bridge. As he started to struggle to his feet, Borgman flew at him and aimed a kick at his head. Tracy dodged. He caught Borgman's foot and twisted, and Borgman flopped over and landed face-down on the bridge.

Tracy jumped to his feet. But Borgman had recovered and was ready for him. They met head-on and grappled, each one struggling to get the advantage. Tracy's foot slipped. He lost his balance for an instant. Borgman thrust forward with all his weight, and Tracy landed against the rail. Instantly, Borgman was on top of him, bending him backwards. He tried to get his fingers at Tracy's eyes. But Tracy got the butt of his right hand under Borgman's chin first. He shoved with all his strength, snapping Borgman's head back. Borgman's hold on him weakened. Tracy kicked, and the kick caught Borgman in a leg, and now it was he who lost his balance. Tracy shoved harder with the hand he had under Borgman's chin. And Borgman tumbled backwards, crashing into the opposite railing.

Weary, Tracy dragged himself back to his feet. But once more Borgman had recovered. He flung himself at Tracy. And Tracy, knowing that if he tried to meet the rush he would be overwhelmed, ducked down and away. Borgman plunged past him—and kept on going, over the railing.

The fall was silent. If Borgman screamed, the sound was drowned out by the roar of the fires. And below the men worked on, unaware of the battle, unaware that it had ended and Borgman had dived into the molten steel. There was no evidence that he had ever existed. The liquid steel had consumed him, leaving no trace.

Tracy stretched out on the bridge, face up, exhausted. The steam from below, the vapor, foamed up around him, concealing him in a cloud. He rested, his eyes closed, horrified by Borgman's terrible death.

After a few more moments, he managed to get to his feet, and he climbed down from the bridge. He found a guard, identified himself, and told him what had happened, then telephoned headquarters. A police car soon arrived for him. He was returned to headquarters, where he made a report, and then he was driven home. He slept, wholly exhausted.

Nine

THE FOLLOWING morning, Tracy conferred with the Chief and Sam and told them in exact detail what had happened the night before.

The Chief said, "Incidentally, I got a call from Dr. Zgani this morning. He wants to call off that press conference."

"I have no objections," Tracy replied. "It was an idea that just didn't work out the way I had hoped."

"It worked," Sam said. "It got you in contact with Computer. It wasn't your fault that it didn't work out *exactly* as you planned it."

"In a sense, it was," Tracy replied. "I should have known that, being able to anticipate me, Computer would realize that Dr. Zgani's announcement was a trick."

"What bothers me is that Computer got away again," the Chief said. "And I don't see how we'll ever be able to find him before it's too late. Unless we suddenly get awfully lucky."

"I don't think we'll have to look for him," Tracy said.

The Chief and Sam looked at him puzzledly.

"You think he's going to turn himself in?" Sam said.

Tracy laughed. "No. But I think he'll come after me. Either that or send someone after me. When Borgman doesn't show up at the meeting place, Computer, of course, is going to realize that he failed to do away with me. He's going to know that Borgman is either dead, or my prisoner."

"So?" the Chief said, leaning forward at his desk.

"Computer thinks I'm a great danger to him," Tracy went on. "He's convinced that as long as I'm alive his plan is threatened. That disturbs him—a great deal. Computer isn't as confident of his powers as he likes to pretend."

"You think he won't be able to proceed until you're out of the way, right?" the Chief said.

Tracy nodded. "He'll try to get me, I believe. And he may be forced to make the attempt himself this time, since he no longer has Borgman to do his dirty work for him. He may have other men—but I doubt it. Right now, I suspect that Computer is working alone."

"What do you plan to do, then?" Sam asked.

"Wait, for one thing," Tracy replied. "Wait for Computer to make his move. And then try to use it to my own advantage."

"I don't know," the Chief said, shaking his head. "With that brain of his, I don't see how anybody can ever get the drop on him."

"He's human, Chief," Tracy said. "He isn't a machine. And, being human, he can make mistakes. Being human, he also has weaknesses."

"Name one," Sam said.

"I've already mentioned one," Tracy replied. "Remember? I told you how flustered, how disturbed, he got when I told him that I'd had somebody follow me, while I was following Dr. Zgani. He said it wouldn't compute. That was the exact word he used."

"I remember. But I don't see the weakness," Sam said.

"Computer was able to anticipate my every move, as long as I functioned in my normal way," Tracy said. "But when I told him I had done something that

I would not normally do—something that I would not logically do—he was upset. Actually, I hadn't done it, of course. But he couldn't be sure of that. That's what I mean about being human, about not having complete confidence in himself. He still has doubts. He doesn't trust his computer mind completely."

"Okay, agreed. But how is that going to help you?" Sam asked.

Tracy leaned back in his chair, scowling. "I'm not sure yet. I think I have an answer. I think I can overcome him by acting illogically—by acting in a way that I would not normally act. But how can I do that? That's the big question."

"Just figure out what you'd do, then don't do it," Sam suggested.

"No. You see, that's a normal—a logical—thought process for me. That makes sense. And, being logical, it's what Computer would expect from me. He'd be prepared for it."

"You're getting a little over my head again," Sam said.

"If I could only stop thinking," Tracy said. "If I could only stop using my mind in an organized and logical way."

"You're asking for a miracle," the Chief said. "A man can't change his whole way of thinking—not overnight, anyway. We'll have to depend on something else to help us catch Computer. Every man on the force is keeping an eye out for him. Maybe he'll turn up."

"Don't count on it," Tracy said. "I suspect he'll stay in hiding. But he'll try to lure me to him. With his mind, I'm sure he's prepared for something like this."

"Then you believe that all we can do is wait? Wait for him to contact us—or you?" the Chief said.

Tracy nodded. "Wait—and try to figure out some way to turn his weakness against him."

Tracy stayed at his desk all through the day, hoping to receive some communication from Computer. He wrestled with the problem of how to revise his normal method of thinking. But there was no approach from Computer. And the problem of altering his thought patterns remained a problem, unsolved.

Sam stopped at his desk late in the afternoon. "I've chased down six leads today," he said. "Men who were sure they'd seen Computer. But they were all wrong."

"That happens," Tracy shrugged.

"I'll tell you," Sam said, dropping into a chair, "I've been thinking about this idea of yours—some way to goof up your way of thinking. And, the more I think about it, the less I think about it. Understand what I mean?"

Tracy smiled and shook his head.

"I mean I've thought about it so much, I can't think about it any more. My brain is empty."

Tracy's eyes narrowed. He looked at Sam interestedly. "That may be it," he said.

"Huh?"

"You said that your brain is empty. That may be it—the way to defeat Computer."

"You're losing me again, Tracy."

"There *is* a way of emptying a mind—we know that," Tracy said. "Gustave Moehler's drug."

"Sure, but why would you—", He interrupted himself. "Anyway, Computer has that drug. He took it from Moehler's laboratory. And Moehler isn't around any more to make a new supply."

"But the formula . . ."

"Do you have it?"

"No," Tracy replied. "But it's just possible that I can find it. It may still be at Moehler's laboratory. Computer took Moehler, and the supply of the drug that was ready. But did he take the formula too? It's possible that he didn't, maybe he didn't need it. Perhaps the existing supply of the drug was all he needed."

"What I don't understand—"

"We'll talk about it in the car," Tracy broke in. "Let's get up to that lab and look around. If I can find that formula . . . ."

He hurried toward the door, and Sam trotted after him. A few minutes later, in Tracy's car, they left the city and drove toward the mountains, where Gustave Moehler's laboratory was located.

"Tracy, what have you got on your mind?" Sam asked, worriedly.

"Remember what Moehler's object was when he developed that drug?"

"Sure. He was looking for a cure for insanity."

"Right. He intended to use it to remove the thoughts that were the basis for the mental illness. But . . . why would it have to be limited to that? Why couldn't *other* thoughts be removed?"

"Sure, why not? What thoughts?"

"I function the way I do because of what I have learned," Tracy replied. "I operate logically because of my experience and what I've been taught. Now . . . if those thoughts, if that reasoning, could be removed . . . Do you see what I'm geting at?"

"You'd be a different person," Sam said, slightly horrified. "Tracy, that would be dangerous."

"Possibly."

"You could destroy yourself!"

"There's always that chance," Tracy admitted. "But, if those thoughts could be removed, why couldn't they also be replaced?"

"You mean just change yourself temporarily?"

"Exactly."

Sam shook his head, dismayed. "Tracy, you'd be playing with something that could . . . I don't know *what* it could do . . . It could make a monster or something out of you."

"I realize—as I said—that there's a risk," Tracy replied. "But, Sam . . . think about it. What will happen if we don't stop Computer?"

"We're not sure."

"No, you're right, we're not entirely positive. But we can speculate. I doubt, frankly, that he could ever get total control of society. But I *don't* doubt that he could gain power over a great many people. And suppose he gained power over our leaders? You can imagine what would happen."

"I know, I know," Sam said. "But Tracy, you've got to think about yourself, too. What about you? This drug of Moehler's is still in the experimental stage. Suppose something went wrong?"

Tracy was silent for a moment. Then he said, "Well . . . maybe we won't find the formula."

They reached the mountain laboratory not long after that. Tracy and Sam tried the doors and windows, but they were still locked.

"That settles it," Sam said. "Let's go back."

Tracy shook his head. He took out his gun and shot the handle off the door.

They entered and turned on the light, and looked around. The laboratory was very well outfitted. At the rear they found Gustave Moehler's living quarters. He had lived very simply. But he had spared no expense when it came to laboratory equipment.

"This is one of the reasons why Computer has to be stopped," Tracy said. "Gustave Moehler was a great scientist. He devoted his whole life, all his energies, to helping other people. And now he's dead. And Computer is the cause of it."

"I know . . . I know all that. But I'm still thinking about you, Tracy. The danger . . ."

Tracy moved on to a desk. "Help me look for the formula," he said.

"What will it look like?"

"I don't know. Just look . . . and hope . . ."

They found nothing in the desk. Next they began searching the files. There were many of them.

"This could take us weeks," Sam grumbled.

"Keep at it."

It was early morning before they finally finished going through all the papers in the files. They had not found the formula for the mind-emptying drug.

"Okay, that settles it," Sam said, relieved. "Whatever you were thinking about doing, you can't do it. Let's go back to headquarters."

Tracy sighed, looking gloomily at the files. "I was sure we would find it. But . . . it's just not here."

"That's what *I* said," Sam grumped, moving toward the exit. "Let's go."

"Be with you in a second," Tracy replied. "I want to take one last look." He headed toward Gustave Moehler's living quarters.

"He wouldn't keep a formula in there!" Sam protested.

But Tracy did not halt.

Sam followed him, and found him in Moehler's

bedroom. He was opening the drawers of a night table.

"See? Nothing," Sam said.

"Yes, apparently . . . Wait a minute—"

Tracy got down on his knees and reached under the bed. He came up clutching a thick sheaf of papers that were bound into a makeshift booklet. He looked at the writing on the top page, then grinned. "I think this is it, Sam."

Tracy began reading. After the first few pages, he smiled broadly. "Yes . . . this is it. The formula is here. Everything is here, a complete record of the experiments."

"That's a great place to keep it, under the bed," Sam said gruffly.

"He was probably reading it in bed and fell asleep and it fell to the floor."

"Why would he be reading it?" Sam asked. "He conducted the experiments, didn't he? Didn't he know what he'd done."

"Sometimes when you're puzzled about something, looking back at what you've done can give you the answer," Tracy replied.

"Puzzled? Puzzled about what? You mean something wasn't working out?"

Tracy shrugged. "I wouldn't know."

"Listen, Tracy, if there's something goofy about that formula, you better stay away from it."

"I didn't say there was anything wrong with it."

"Play it safe, Tracy!"

"We'll see . . ."

They left the laboratory. On the way back, Sam drove. And Tracy, with the car's interior light on, read the papers he had found.

"It wasn't that Moehler was puzzled," Tracy said

after a while. "I think he had found something—a new characteristic of the drug. The figures here seem to indicate that."

"Like what?"

"The effect of the drug may not necessarily last for twenty-four hours," Tracy replied. "He was using a certain amount of it for each injection, and the effect always lasted for twenty-four hours, to the second. But, during one experiment, by mistake, he used a little less of the drug. And the effect lasted for a shorter period of time."

"Was he sure?"

"He hadn't carried out any further experiments along that line," Tracy replied. "But he intended to. He had worked out a theoretical chart, indicating how long the effect of the drug would last, according to the size of the dosage."

"Theoretical?"

"He was guessing. He intended to begin experimenting to find out if his guess was correct."

"Why didn't he?"

"That was probably when Computer had him kidnapped."

"Tracy, I've said it a dozen times, and I say it again—don't play with that stuff!"

"I'm not playing, Sam."

"Don't touch it!"

"I'll think about it," Tracy replied.

The following morning, Tracy met with the Chief and Sam again. The Chief was in a cranky mood.

"We've been waiting, and nothing has happened," he said. "We haven't had any contact from Computer. I think we better take some action."

"Right," Sam said.

"What exactly shall we do?" Tracy smiled.

"That's what we've got to talk about," the Chief replied. "Does anybody have any ideas?"

"Let's broadcast a general alarm," Sam said. "Let's get everybody looking for him."

"And start a panic?" Tracy said. "Besides, I think it would be pointless. Computer isn't going to show himself."

"He isn't going to contact us, either," the Chief said.

"I think he will."

The Chief groaned. "All right—suppose he does. What then? Have you figured that out?"

"I hope so," Tracy replied. "I have a plan."

"I was afraid of that," Sam said.

The Chief looked at Sam, then at Tracy. "Well?"

Tracy told him about going to Gustave Moehler's laboratory and finding the formula for the mind-emptying drug. He explained about Moehler's notes on his experiments.

"I want to try an experiment on myself," he said. "I want to try to remove the thoughts from my mind that make me think and act the way I do."

"Change yourself?" the Chief said, obviously disturbed by the idea.

"Yes, make myself into a different person," Tracy replied. "If I can do that, then—theoretically—Computer won't be able to anticipate my every move."

The Chief shook his head. "I'm against it."

"Hear me out," Tracy said. "This is the way I intend to do it. I'll inject myself with the drug, then, as I empty my mind, Sam will record my thoughts on tape. After that, he will play the thoughts back into my mind. And I'll be able to think logically again."

"You'll be right back where you started," the Chief said.

"No. I'll have that tape of my thoughts. I can play it and select the thoughts that control my method of thinking."

"Yeah?"

"I'll make notes of what those thoughts are," Tracy went on. "Then we'll do the whole thing over again. I'll inject myself with the drug, I'll empty my mind, and Sam will put the thoughts on tape. But, before he plays them back to me again, he will remove those thoughts that control my present way of thinking."

"I understand it, but I'm still against it," the Chief said. "What'll that make you? What'll you be?"

"For the most part, I'll be the same person," Tracy replied. "But one important thing will be missing. I won't have the thought process that guides me now—the thinking that makes me function logically."

"How *will* you function—if at all?" Sam asked.

"By instinct," Tracy replied.

"I'm not sure I get that," the Chief frowned.

"As it is," Tracy explained, "I think and then I act. But, without my reasoning to guide me, I'll act *without* thinking—instinctively. The odds are that I won't do what I would normally do."

"And that will keep Computer from knowing what you're going to do before you do it?"

"I hope so."

"I see a problem," the Chief said. "The effect of the drug lasts for twenty-four hours. Suppose while you're under the influence of the drug, Computer makes the contact with us? You won't be able to do anything about it."

Tracy then told the Chief about Gustave Moehler's theory that the time of the drug's effectiveness could be limited by controlling the dosage. "In other words," he said, "if I take a certain amount, the effect will last a certain time. If I take more, the effect will last longer, and if I take less, the effect will continue for a shorter period of time."

"That's what he thought—but he wasn't sure—right?"

"It makes sense," Tracy replied.

"But it's still a theory—he hadn't tested it."

"Yes, that's right. But I'll just have to take the chance. I'll inject myself with enough of the drug to keep me under its influence for—oh, a few hours—and just hope that it works out that way. We don't have time to prove that the theory is right or wrong."

"I don't like it. I don't like anything about it," Sam said.

The Chief sighed. "I'm not too crazy about it myself," he said. "But, on the other hand, Computer is a danger to everybody. And . . . we're pretty sure that the drug won't harm Tracy. It didn't hurt any of the other men who were injected with it."

"That isn't the danger," Sam pointed out. "The danger is that Tracy won't be able to act the way he usually does. What will he do? When he's face to face with Computer—if that ever happens—how will he react?" He turned to Tracy. "What will you do? What will happen?"

"I just don't know," Tracy replied.

"See? The whole thing is so unpredictable."

"I know. But I have to take the chance," Tracy said. He faced the Chief. "What do you say?"

The Chief got up and walked to the window and stood with his back to Tracy and Sam, considering. "It's a big, big risk," he mused.

"Chief, being a policeman is a risk," Tracy pointed

out. "Every time I leave headquarters to investigate a case, I'm taking a risk. That's my life."

"Yes . . . but this . . ." He turned back to them. "All right, Tracy, if you want to do it. I'll trust your judgement."

Tracy got to his feet. "Good. I'm going back to Moehler's laboratory now. He has the elements to produce the drug there. I'll make up a supply of it, then come back here and—" He grinned at Sam. "—and then we can get to work."

"All right, I'll do it," Sam said. "But I won't like it."

Tracy headed for the door, then halted. "There's a telephone out there at the lab," he said. "If we hear from Computer, get on the line to me immediately."

The Chief nodded. "Good luck."

It was late afternoon when Tracy returned from Gustave Moehler's laboratory. He had mixed a supply of the mind-emptying drug, and he had it with him, along with a needle with which to inject it.

He asked Sam if there had been any contact with Computer.

"Nothing," Sam replied. "Tracy, I'll bet he's left the country or something. Wouldn't that be the intelligent thing to do, if he thinks you're a danger to him? Sure. So, let's skip this other business."

Tracy shook his head. "He wouldn't leave the country—not for long, anyway. I'm sure, Sam, that he has doubts about his plan. He won't proceed until he's positive that I'm out of the way."

"Then look at it this way. Suppose—"

"Sam, I'm going through with this," Tracy broke in. "You can't talk me out of it."

"All right," Sam sighed gloomily. "What next?"

"Get a couple of tape recorders."

"Two?"

"I suspect I'll do a lot of talking," Tracy replied. "While one machine is recording, you can be getting the next one ready to take over when the first one runs out of tape."

"Oh . . . yeah, I see."

Sam departed to get the recorders, and Tracy moved on to an interrogation room. He placed the holder that contained the vials of drug and the other equipment on the table, then opened it and began preparing an injection. A few moments later, Sam arrived with the recorders.

"Lock the door," Tracy said. "We want privacy."

"I guess so," Sam replied, "if you're going to tell these machines everything you know." From the door, which he was locking, he glanced back at Tracy. "Uh . . . is there anything you might not want me to hear?"

Tracy laughed. "I can't think of anything." He held the needle up to the light, making sure that it registered the amount of the drug that he wanted.

"Tracy, how about thinking this over just once more," Sam said, returning.

"Are the machines ready?"

"Sleep on it," Sam pleaded. "You'll probably change your mind. Or maybe—"

"Sam—the machines."

"Okay."

Sam readied the tape recorders. Finally, he said, "All set when you are."

"If Moehler's theory is right," Tracy said, "I've used enough of the drug to keep me under its influence for five hours. That should be enough time. I've studied Moehler's notes on his experiments and five hours was usually long enough for the subject to empty his mind completely. You understand what you're to do, don't you, after I stop talking?"

"Right. I play it back to you."

"Okay, then. . ."

"Tracy. . ."

Tracy shook his head. "Let's not discuss it any more, Sam."

Sam nodded.

Tracy injected himself with the drug. A vacant look came into his eyes. He sat, staring blankly ahead. Nervously, Sam waited.

But nothing happened. Tracy did not speak.

"Tracy!"

Tracy's head turned. He faced Sam. But still he said nothing.

"Tracy! Talk to me!"

Tracy's mouth moved, forming a word. But it was not understandable. And he said no more.

Sam had a sudden inspiration. Tracy had responded to all of his commands. Maybe all he had to do was—

"Tracy! Tell me your thoughts—all of your thoughts!"

That was all that was needed. Words poured from Tracy. He spoke rapidly, unaware of what he was doing, unaware even of what he was saying. He was like a machine.

Sam looked at his watch. It was a few minutes after four in the afternoon. Tracy would be under the influence of the drug—if Moehler's theory was correct—until at least nine in the evening.

Time dragged on, and Tracy continued to babble. After a while, Sam stopped listening.

Then, a little after eight that evening, Tracy abruptly stopped talking. It was as if his switch had been suddenly turned off. At first, Sam was startled and afraid. But then he realized what had happened. Tracy had completed the process. He had revealed every thought that was in his mind.

Sam removed the tapes, then prepared them to be played back. Tracy was still under the influence of the drug, still staring vacantly into space. Now, Moehler's theory would be tested. Would Tracy come out of the spell at the expected time?

At nine o'clock exactly, Tracy suddenly blinked his eyes. The theory was correct.

"Tracy . . . ?" Sam said.

But there was no reply. Tracy could not think. His mind was completely empty.

Quickly, Sam injected him with a second dose of the drug. And, as before, Tracy's eyes became blank, and he stiffened, as if in a state of shock.

Sam switched on the first tape recorder. And for the second time he listened to Tracy's thoughts as they were played back into his mind.

Once more, time proceeded at a snail's pace. Sam felt hungry. He picked up the telephone and ordered food from the nearby restaurant. When it was delivered, an officer brought it to him. He ate listlessly, half listening, half not listening to the drone of Tracy's voice as it came from the recorder.

It was about one-thirty in the morning when the tape finally ran out. For another half-hour, Sam sat and waited for the effect of the drug to wear off. And then, right on schedule, Tracy blinked his eyes again, coming out of the spell.

"Nothing's happening," Tracy said. "It isn't working."

"You're okay!" Sam grinned happily.

"What? Of course I'm all right. But the drug isn't working."

"It worked," Sam told him. He pointed to the clock on the wall. "Look at the time. Where have you been for the past ten hours if it didn't work?"

"Amazing!" Tracy said. "I wasn't aware of anything. Did I talk?"

Sam put his hands to his head. "Aiii, did you talk!"

"All right, let's get at it," Tracy said. "Put those tapes on again. I want to hear everything I said, and edit out the parts that make me function the way I do."

Sam started the tapes playing once more. And for the third time he found himself listening to Tracy's thoughts.

"Tracy, if you don't mind, I think I'll get in a little shut-eye," Sam said.

"Go ahead. I'll wake you when I'm ready."

The editing job took almost six hours. It was eight in the morning by then. Tracy heard sounds in the corridor—the men on day duty were coming in. There was a knock at the door. When he opened it, he found the Chief outside.

"Everything okay?" the Chief asked.

Tracy smiled. "Everything but Sam. He's sick."

"Sick?"

"Sick of hearing me babble," Tracy replied. "And now he has to suffer through it again."

Tracy explained what had been accomplished so far. Then he and the Chief walked down the corridor to the room where Sam was napping and woke him.

"Ready," Tracy said.

"I'm hungry again," Sam complained.

"You're stalling."

"No. I'm committed to this now. But I'm hungry."

"All right. I guess I am too," Tracy said. "Get us some breakfast. I'll have toast and coffee."

"You realize, of course," the Chief said to Tracy," if we don't get in contact with Computer this is all going to be a waste of time. No word from him yet?"

Tracy shook his head.

Sam put down the phone. "Breakfast is on the way up. Have you finished, Tracy? Have you removed all the thoughts that make you think the way you do?"

"I think so . . . I hope so."

"Well, I'll leave you," the Chief said. "If you want me . . . well, you know where I am." He walked on down the corridor.

"Let's go back to our lab," Tracy said to Sam.

When they reached there, Tracy showed Sam a tape. "This is the one you're to play back to me next time," he said. "All the thoughts that control my logical thinking have been removed."

Sam took it gingerly. "Boy, I better not lose it."

"There's no reason for it to leave this room," Tracy said.

Sam placed the tape on the table. "I'll watch it close, anyway. No telling–"

There was a knock at the door. "Food!" a voice called in.

Sam opened the door and took the tray from the officer who had brought it. Then he locked the door again, and he and Tracy sat down to eat.

"I'm getting a little scared again," Sam said. "Tracy, when your mind was empty you were like . . . like I don't know what . . . like a blob . . ."

"Don't worry about it."

"But, just suppose . . . I mean, how do we know how you'll be when part of you is missing? Maybe you won't be able to do anything. I don't even like to think about it."

"Then don't," Tracy replied grimly. "Eat. We have work to do."

Ten

IT WAS A little after nine that morning when they finished eating. Tracy immediately injected himself with the mind-emptying drug. Grimly Sam began the long hours of listening. Then, a little after two in the afternoon he started playing back the tape that Tracy had edited earlier. Less time was required for this step in the process, since a great many of Tracy's thoughts were missing. It was a few minutes before six in the evening when the final words of the tape were played. Sam had to wait until a short time after seven before Tracy became aware again.

Tracy's eyes blinked. "Is it over?" he asked.

Sam nodded wearily. "Can we eat now?"

"We just had breakfast," Tracy replied, surprised.

"That was this morning, Tracy. It's night now."

"Oh . . . oh, yes . . . I forgot. When you're not conscious of the passing time, it's difficult to . . . well . . . I guess I'm hungry too."

"You don't seem any different," Sam said. "Maybe it didn't work."

Tracy looked bothered. "I don't feel any different either," he said. "What I mean is, I seem to be thinking the same. I hope this all hasn't been a waste of time."

"Well, I won't be unhappy if it didn't work," Sam said. "I didn't like the idea in the first place." He picked up the phone. "What do you want to eat?"

A look of mild puzzlement passed across Tracy's face.

"Tracy? What do you want for dinner?"

"I–I don't know."

Sam peered at him. His face was suddenly covered with perspiration. "Tracy? Are you okay?"

"Yes . . . I . . . Sam, I can't decide . . ."

"You mean you don't know what you want for dinner? A simple thing like– Oh-oh."

Tracy nodded. "This is the result, apparently. When I removed the thoughts that controlled my way of thinking, I evidently removed the ability to make a decision too. Sam, you'll have to stay with me every minute. You'll have to make my decisions for me."

The color drained from Sam's face. The idea that Tracy had just suggested appalled him. Suppose he made the *wrong* decision? And suppose, as the result of it, Tracy were killed?

"No. No, Tracy, I can't do that. It's too dangerous."

"It's the only way, Sam. Sam, I need you now."

"No, Tracy. Give yourself another injection. Those thoughts that you need, let me play them back to you. Okay?"

Tracy peered at him worriedly. "Is that what I should do? You'll have to tell me, Sam. I can't decide."

But Sam didn't want to make the decision either. After all, they had spent a lot of time getting Tracy into this condition. It was what Tracy had wanted.

Sam picked up the phone again. "I'll get the Chief in here," he said. "Let him decide."

The Chief arrived a few minutes later. Sam told him what had happened, then said, "I want to put those thoughts back into his mind, so he can make his own decisions. I can't be responsible."

"You'll have to, Sam," the Chief said. "Tracy knew something like this was going to happen. He was willing to take the chance." He turned to Tracy. "You want Sam to make your decisions for you—right?"

"I—I don't know," Tracy replied.

"See?" Sam said, troubled. "Suppose Computer makes contact with us? Suppose . . . I don't know . . . suppose, whatever happens after that, suppose Tracy is in danger. How will I know what to do?"

"That's the reason for this," the Chief replied. "Don't you see, Sam? Tracy will have to rely on instinct. If he gets into a dangerous situation, he won't be able to think his way out of it—and, because of that, Computer won't be able to anticipate what he'll do."

"But, Chief—"

"Sam, this is what Tracy wants. Stick by him. Stay with him every second. Make his decisions for him."

"All right," Sam said gloomily. "But I'm afraid to think what might happen."

The Chief left. Sam ordered food for himself and Tracy. It arrived soon after that, and they sat across the table from each other, eating, not saying much.

"Boy, I'm bushed," Sam said, finally. "I could use about twenty-four hours sleep. How about you?"

"I don't know, Sam. I'm tired. But, I don't know. Should I sleep?"

"Yeah, I think we both better—"

There was a knock at the door. When Sam answered it he found an officer there.

"A kid outside," the officer said. "He wants to talk to Tracy. He has a message for him, he says."

Sam shook his head. "Tracy can't talk to anybody now. Tell him— Wait a minute!" He turned to Tracy. "That might be a message from Computer." He faced back to the officer. "Send the kid in," he said.

The officer departed.

"Tracy, this could be it," Sam said. "If it is, you were right about Computer—he's not as sure of himself as he pretended to be."

A few moments later, the officer returned. He had a teenage boy with him.

"I'll take that message," Sam said to the boy.

The boy hesitated. "Are you Mr. Tracy?"

"No, but—"

"The guy gave me a couple bucks and told me to give the message to Mr. Tracy—and *only* Mr. Tracy," the boy said.

Sam turned to Tracy. "Tell him it's okay, to give me the message," he said.

Tracy nodded obediently, then asked the boy to turn over the message to Sam.

The boy produced a fold of paper from his pocket and handed it to Sam. Sam read:

> My dear Mr. Tracy:
>
> I find it difficult to proceed, knowing that you are pursuing me. Consequently, I would like to bargain with you. I think that my plan can be altered slightly so that it would be of benefit to both of us. If you are willing to discuss the matter, you have only to indicate your agreement, and I will make arrangements for us to meet, face to face.
>
> I do not intend to be tricked, however. If your answer is yes to this request, all you have to do to let me know is send this boy home. I will be watching. If your answer is no—then I will have no choice but to destroy you.
>
> Computer

"That's it," Sam said. "What do we do now, Tracy?"

"Well . . ." Tracy hesitated. Then, apologetically, he said, "You'll have to decide, Sam."

Sam read the note again, scowling. Then he spoke to the boy. "How did you get this?" he said.

"I was walking along the street, about a block from here, when this guy drove up in this car," the boy replied. "He told me he had this message he wanted me to deliver, and he'd give me a couple bucks."

"What kind of car? What was the license number?"

The boy shrugged. "I didn't pay much attention."

"He was a block away, and we didn't even know it," Sam grumbled.

"He must still be around somewhere," Tracy said. "He's evidently watching, waiting for the boy to leave. According to the note, that's how I'm supposed to answer, yes or no."

"Right—he must be parked somewhere nearby," Sam said. "Maybe we can still catch him. But then . . . maybe he's in one of the buildings across the street. He could have put the car somewhere and—" He groaned. "The fact is, we don't know where he might be. He wouldn't make it easy for us. He wouldn't park outside headquarters."

"Do you want me any more?" the boy asked.

"Just hold it a minute," Sam replied. "I have to think this out. What would Tracy do?"

The boy glanced toward Tracy. "I thought you said that's who he is," he said.

"He is. But he can't— Nevermind, it's a long story."

Sam sat down at the table. He slumped, pulling at his chin, puzzling. "All he wants from us right now is a yes or no," he said, speaking to Tracy. "Maybe we better tell him yes, then see what we can think up after that. At least, that way, we'll keep him on the hook. What do you say?"

"I'm sorry, Sam, I can't help."

Sam addressed the boy. "Okay, you go home now," he said. "Go straight home, understand?"

"That's where I was going anyway."

"Okay—do it!"

The boy and the officer left.

"Well, all we can do now is wait until we hear from Computer again," Sam said. "And who knows when that will be? I don't like this—this playing games with characters like Computer. He isn't interested in bargaining. He knows he can't get a deal out of you, Tracy. So, what is he up to?"

"I don't know," Tracy replied. "I can think of several things. But I can't decide which possibility to prepare for."

"Well, one thing," Sam sighed, "this can't go on like this forever. Sooner or later, one way or another, it's got to end. In the meantime—" He yawned. "Let's try to get some sleep."

It was the following evening before they heard from Computer again. They were in the interrogation room, waiting, when the phone rang and the officer on the switchboard told them that there was a call for Tracy.

"Hold it," Sam said to the officer. "We're moving into another office, where there's an extension."

The Chief had left for the day, so they used his office. Sam picked up the phone and told the officer to put the call through, then he signalled for Tracy to pick up the extension.

"Yes? This is Tracy . . ."

"Ahhh . . . Mr. Tracy," said Computer. "I hope I haven't kept you waiting too long. I assume that you are anxious to discuss terms with me."

"I don't know. What did you have in mind?"

"It isn't the sort of thing one likes to discuss on the telephone, is it?" Computer asked smoothly. "Are you prepared to meet me?"

(Sam, listening on the other phone, signalled to Tracy to reply in the affirmative)

"Yes," Tracy responded, after a moment.

"Excellent! Now then, follow my instructions. Do you know where Hollow Tree Road is?"

"No."

"I think you will be able to find someone who can direct you to it. I want you to follow Hollow Tree Road, driving east, until you come to Pine Woods Road. I will meet you at the point where the two roads cross. I will not be there when you get there, but I will arrive some time after that. You are to wait for me. Do you understand?"

Tracy said, "Yes—at the juncture of Hollow Tree Road and Pine Woods Road. And I'm to wait for you."

"Correct. And you must come alone," Computer warned. "I will be watching. If I see that you are accompanied by someone else, I will not meet you. Clear?"

"I understand," Tracy murmured.

"When you reach the place, get out of your car. Stand a few yards from it. In time, I will join you."

"When?"

"When I choose to join you," Computer snapped. "I won't tell you how long you will have to wait. I want to be sure that you are alone and that you are not being followed by a squad of your men."

Tracy said, "What I meant was, when shall I leave for the meeting place?"

"As soon as our conversation ends. Do you have any more questions?"

(Sam shook his head vehemently, signalling for Tracy to reply in the negative.)

"No." Tracy said.

"Then, goodbye for now, Mr. Tracy. We will be meeting again very soon."

Then the line went dead.

"That's easy enough," Sam said, hanging up. "I know the spot he was talking about. There used to be a factory of some kind—a glass factory, I think—at that spot. If I remember right, it's closed now. That's probably where he's hiding—inside that glass factory."

"What are we going to do?" Tracy asked.

"Oh, boy, that's the thing," Sam sighed. "What would *you* do, if you knew what you were doing? Would you string along with him? Would you do what he wants? Or would you take a raiding party out to that glass factory?"

Tracy looked at him helplessly.

"I know—you don't know," Sam replied. "The problem is, maybe he *isn't* hiding-out in that old glass factory. Maybe he's watching from somewhere nearby. That would make more sense. And if we sent a lot of men out to that factory, and Computer saw them, that might goof up the whole works."

"Evidently we don't have a choice," Tracy said. "We have to do exactly what Computer told us to do."

"Not exactly. I can't send you out there alone. I'm going with you."

"Won't that—as you say—goof up the works, too?"

"I'll stay out of sight," Sam replied. "I'll duck down in the back seat of the car. He won't see me."

"Would I let you do that if I could make the decision?" Tracy asked.

"How do I know? Probably not. You'd probably decide to go out there alone. But this is different—I don't know what you'll do when you come face to face with Computer. You're not exactly yourself, you know, Tracy."

"Just asking," Tracy smiled.

Sam explained to Tracy how to get to the junction of Hollow Tree Road and Pine Woods Road. Then they left the building and got into Tracy's car, with Tracy at the wheel, and Sam hunched down on the floor in back.

Following Sam's directions, Tracy drove out of the city by way of the main highway. About a half-hour after he had passed the city limits he came to the turn off to Hollow Tree Road, then drove east. The road was dark. Tracy could see the lights of a few farm houses in the distance.

"He sure picked a good spot," Sam said from the rear seat. "There won't be anybody within shouting distance of that place at this time of night."

"Unless that factory is still operating," Tracy pointed out.

"I'm about one-hundred per cent positive that it isn't," Sam replied. "And, anyway, it wouldn't be open at night."

"There might be a guard."

"Tracy don't count on it. Don't count on anything. I'll be here. But, according to what Computer said, he wants you to get out of the car. So, you're going to be pretty much on your own." He was silent for a second, then he said, "Do you want to turn back?"

Tracy glanced back, then faced front again. "Whatever you say, Sam. You're making the decisions."

"Don't remind me. I keep thinking I'm going to make a mistake. In fact, maybe I already have."

"I think we're getting there," Tracy said. "I see a sign post up ahead. It looks like the other road. Yes, and there's the factory building. I can see a dark shape. It looks closed and deserted all right."

"When you get to the place where the roads meet, pull over to the side," Sam said. "But don't turn off the motor. Let's see what we can see first. We might want to make a fast getaway."

Tracy slowed the car. When he reached the junction, he pulled over, as Sam had suggested, then let the motor idle.

"See anything?" Sam asked.

"It's pretty dark." Tracy squinted toward the factory building. "I don't see anything over there," he reported. "It looks abandoned. There's a reflection of moonlight . . . the windows appear to be broken."

"Is there another car around anywhere?"

"Not that I can see. But there could be one behind the factory."

"Where else could Computer be hiding?" Sam asked. "He must be around somewhere. He said he'd be watching."

"Maybe that was a bluff."

"Maybe. But maybe not, too. Is there a hill around anywhere? Anyplace high?"

"No, I . . . Wait, yes, I think I can see the outline of a hill . . . or a mound. It's over to the right. He might be parked on Pine Woods Road, watching us from there. Isn't that possible?"

"From where I am, anything could be possible," Sam replied. "I can't see anything."

"What should I do?" Tracy asked.

Sam did not reply for a moment. Then, reluctantly, he replied, "I guess we better follow through on the instructions. Get out of the car. But stand close to it—in case you have to jump in. I just don't like any part of this. Computer has something in mind—and it isn't bargaining."

Tracy opened the car door and stepped out and closed the door behind him.

"Can you see anything now?" Sam asked.

"The same."

"Okay. All you can do is—"

A shot rang out. A bullet hit the hood of the car and then went screaming off into nowhere. At the sound of the shot, Tracy instinctively dived toward the ditch at the side of the road. He hit the dirt and rolled into the ditch.

"Tracy!" Sam shouted, popping up from the rear seat. "Did he get you!"

Tracy had flattened himself in the dirt. "I'm okay!" he called back.

"Where did the shot come from? Did you see?"

"I didn't see a thing," Tracy replied. "I just heard it—and jumped."

"From that mound, I think," Sam said. "That would be the safest place for him—out in the open, but with a barrier to hide behind. Let's get out of here. Get back in the car."

Tracy rose up from the ditch. But as his head and shoulders appeared another shot cracked in the darkness. It kicked up dirt in front of Tracy. Once more, he flattened himself in the trench.

"Stay there!" Sam commanded. "I thought I saw a flash that time. I think—I'm not sure—but I think it came from the direction of that mound. I'm going after him, Tracy. Just stay right where you are. Okay? Clear?"

"Whatever you say," Tracy replied.

For a moment, all was silent. Then Tracy heard a car door quietly close. He guessed that Sam had slipped out of the car and was making his way toward the mound.

Suddenly, more shots—one, two, three, four, in rapid succession—barked viciously in the night. They dug holes in the ditch around Tracy. Computer, apparently, had somehow guessed or discovered where he was hiding.

Without thinking about what he was doing, Tracy leaped up and bolted. He dashed forward, following the ditch. More shots spat out at him. A bullet tore through his sleeve. He hit the ground again, and lay there panting, gripped by a kind of animal panic. One thought raced through his mind—he needed shelter.

Another shot tore through the night, whining, and kicking up dirt behind him. Tracy jumped up and ran toward the factory building, driven by the frantic need for a sanctuary. The only sound as he raced toward the building was the sound of his own footfalls. The fact bothered him. Why were there no shots? But instinct drove him on.

He reached the building and pressed himself against the wall. Now, there was almost complete silence. A few yards ahead he saw an opening—a door. Quickly, he moved on, reached the door, then slipped inside the building. He found himself lighted by a ray of moonlight. But before he could move on, a voice cracked at him out of the darkness inside the building.

"Tracy! Don't move an inch!"

Tracy froze. It was Computer's voice.

"Your weapon!" Computer ordered. "Throw it in front of you—into the darkness. Quick!"

Unable to resist, Tracy reached inside his jacket, got his pistol, then tossed it forward. It clattered on the floor.

Computer's voice came from out of the darkness again. "Well . . . my plan is working, although not exactly as I conceived it. I didn't really expect you to get this far, Mr. Tracy. But my aim with a rifle is apparently not perfect. No matter, however. I have you now. I have you in my sight. And here, in this abandoned building, you will die."

Thoughts raced through Tracy's mind, each thought telling him to try a different means of escape. But he could not choose. The thoughts ran head-on into each other, becoming a spaghetti of useless notions.

"What? No defiance, Mr. Tracy?" Computer said. "Defy me! I expect it. I insist!"

But Tracy only stared vacantly into the darkness.

"Mr. Tracy, you forget—I know your mind. That's how I got you here. I knew you could not resist. Now—prove me right again. Defy me, Mr. Tracy!"

Tracy sensed concern in Computer's tone. Instinct told him that Computer was off-guard. Taking advantage of the situation, he plunged forward into the darkness. The gun flashed—but the shots missed him.

Tracy charged headlong into the blackness. The gun spoke again. The bullets hit—but nowhere near Tracy. Ahead, he saw a glint of light. He raced toward it—and then found himself in another section of the building. Moonlight, filtering in through holes in the roof was reflected all around. Tracy halted, fascinated by the sight. It was as if he had entered a room of mirrors. And then he understood. This was evidently a storage room, a left-over from the days when the building had been a glass factory. Almost mesmerized, he moved forward. Abruptly he was confronted by hundreds of images of himself—his own reflection in many, many, many sheets of glass.

A shot rang out again. There was a shattering sound as a sheet of glass—and Tracy's reflection in it—suddenly disappeared.

"I see you!" Computer's voice raged somewhere behind Tracy.

Tracy stepped aside, moving out of the doorway. At the same instant, his reflection moved. And now he could see himself pressed against a wall, waiting—a trapped animal.

Another shot—another pane of glass disintegrated.

"Which one are you!" Computer's voice raged at the images.

There was a furious volley of shots. Reflections disappeared as if by magic.

"Kill!" Computer screamed madly.

The sounds of shots and shattering glass was deafening.

Then silence. And Tracy's reflection still stood, taunting, as if Tracy were immortal.

"Kill! Kill! Kill!"

There was a panic in Computer's voice. More shots, fired wildly, sprayed the storeroom, and more images disappeared.

Then Tracy saw a new reflection in the sheets of glass—Sam's. It was a small reflection, as if Sam were far in the distance.

"No!" Computer screamed. "What are you? Who are you!"

The reflection of Sam raised a gun and fired.

There was no sound of shattering glass this time. Only a dull thud as a bullet bit into a wooden beam.

"Kill!" Computer shrieked. "Kill! Ki–"

The shriek ended abruptly. It was followed by a strangling sound–then a crash, the sound of something heavy falling. After that, there was silence.

Sam's reflection grew larger–he seemed to be approaching.

"Tracy! Where are you?"

"Here!" Tracy stepped out into the opening. "Did you get him?"

"He's got," Sam replied. "But I didn't do it."

Tracy saw Sam's silhouette and moved toward him. "What happened?"

"He just stopped shooting all of a sudden and dropped," Sam replied.

Tracy saw Computer then. He was lying on the floor, on his back. His eyes were closed. His rifle was lying useless beside him. Tracy bent down to examine him.

"Dead," Tracy said. "But you didn't shoot him, Sam."

Sam shook his head. "I couldn't see him in the dark. I fired–but I heard my bullet hit wood. After that, I heard him yell. He was screaming 'Kill!' Then, blooey, I don't know–I heard him drop."

"I don't understand it, either," Tracy said. He put a hand to his forehead. "My mind . . . it's . . . I'm so confused about so many things . . ."

"Let's get out of here," Sam said. "I've got some thoughts back at headquarters that I want to put back into your head."

"What about him?"

"We'll send a wagon for him," Sam replied.

They made their way out of the building, to Tracy's car. This time, Sam got behind the wheel. A few moments later they were driving back toward the city.

"Anyway, I'll say this—I don't know how, but your idea worked," Sam said.

"My idea?" Tracy replied, troubled. "I can't seem— Thinking is very difficult."

"Just take it easy," Sam said. "Rest. Don't try to think."

When they reached headquarters, Sam hurried Tracy to the interrogation room. He locked the door, then injected Tracy with the mind-emptying drug. A moment later, Tracy began expelling his thoughts.

Sam arranged for Computer's body to be picked up. Then he telephoned the Chief at his home, awakening him, and asked him to come to headquarters. The Chief arrived about three-quarters of an hour later. With Tracy's voice in the background, Sam told the Chief what had happened.

"Tracy had it figured out right," the Chief said.

"I guess so. But I don't know exactly how. Anyway, that isn't important now. What worries me is Tracy. He was having trouble—he couldn't seem to think at all."

The Chief glanced at Tracy. "He'll be all right," he said. But he did not sound very sure of himself.

The hours dragged by. The Chief and Sam sat listening to Tracy as he talked on. And then finally he fell silent. He peered blankly into space.

"That's it," Sam said. "Now, I play back that other tape, the one with all his thoughts on it."

"Everything? The thoughts that control his method of thinking?"

"Everything," Sam nodded.

Sam started the tape machine going. It was almost eight in the morning by then. Outside the door there were sounds of movement as the men on the day duty arrived and the men on night duty departed.

For the next four hours and some minutes the machine played on. The Chief left the room and went to his office to begin taking care of his day's obligations. Sam sat slumped in a chair, or paced the room, half-listening to the taped sound of Tracy's voice, half thinking his own thoughts, worrying about the outcome.

The tape ended. But there was no reaction from Tracy, since he was still under the influence of the drug. He simply sat, staring vacantly. Sam sighed deeply, waiting patiently for the time to pass.

The door opened and the Chief came back in. He dropped into another chair and peered at Tracy hopefully.

"How much longer?" the Chief asked.

"Any minute now."

"Sam ... if this doesn't work out right ... what I mean is, if this—"

Tracy's eyes flickered. He stirred. Then his eyes brightened.

"Tracy ... ?"

He looked at Sam. "Where have I— Oh, yes, I remember now." He smiled. "I remember everything."

Sam grinned broadly.

"Are you sure you're all right?" the Chief said to Tracy.

"I think so—except, I'm hungry. When do we eat around here?"

"What would you like?" Sam asked.

Tracy rattled off an order.

"He's back to normal! He can think!" Sam shouted gleefully. He reached for the phone to call in an order. "This is the—"

But as he reached for it, the phone rang. He picked up the receiver, talked for a few moments, then hung up. "That was the hospital," he said to Tracy. "They finished the autopsy on Computer. He had some kind of a brain hemorrhage."

"A what?" the Chief said.

"It was almost like his brain blew up," Sam replied. "Anyway, that's what the hospital said."

The Chief turned to Tracy. "Does that mean anything to you?"

"It doesn't surprise me," Tracy replied. "A lot of things were happening that were confusing him. For one thing, he couldn't figure out my behavior. I wasn't functioning the way he thought I ought to. I didn't seem to know exactly what I was doing—and that wasn't like me. Then I blundered into that room with all the sheets of glass. And he saw all of those images of me. The confusion was compounded."

"When I finally got there, he sounded like he was off his head," Sam said.

"Seeing you was the last straw, I think," Tracy said. "He assumed that I would be alone. And I would have been if I'd been functioning normally. That was too much for him. Nothing was working out the way he'd planned it. It wasn't . . . well, it wasn't computing."

"You mean it was all too much for his brain to handle and it just exploded from the overload?" Sam said.

Tracy smiled. "Who would believe that?"

"Not me," the Chief said. "Not if I heard it from somebody else."

"How else can it be explained?" Sam said.

"The hospital was satisfied with its diagnosis, wasn't

it?" Tracy said. "Let's just leave it at that. Let's say he had a brain hemorrhage."

"But—" Sam began.

"If we told anybody what we think happened, they'd say we were out of our minds," the Chief pointed out.

Sam glanced at the container of mind-emptying drug and then at the tape recorder. "Couldn't you phrase that some other way, Chief?" he said, wincing.